RAZOR'S EDGE
6
CHRONICLES

CHAINED
BY
MEMORY

CELINE JEANJEAN

ISBN: 9782492523298

Cover by: bonobobookcovers.com
Editing by: copybykath.com

CLICK HERE TO JOIN MY NEWSLETTER

AND RECEIVE THESE FREE STORIES

Subscribe to Celine Jeanjean's newsletter and receive these
three novellas for free!

Go to:

http://celinejeanjean.com/razor-bonus

1

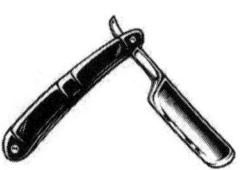

Bearing in mind that Sarroch is the CEO of a large company, when he said he had a plane, I had certain expectations. I'm not a princess, so it's not like I expect the height of luxury when I travel. But I *do* expect something from this century, at least, especially when I'm flying in the private plane of the CEO of one of Panong's largest companies.

Instead, what I got is a small rust bucket that would have looked like it had seen better days during World War II. I don't *actually* know if it's old enough to have been around back then—I'm not one of those plane nerds—but it sure looks that way to me.

And more importantly, it feels like that, too.

For starters, the plane has a propeller. Flying over the Himalayas in something that requires a *propeller* really doesn't inspire confidence. The cockpit is narrow enough to make a budget airline economy seat feel roomy, so Sarroch and I are crammed in there next to each other with our knees making a decent attempt at reaching our ears.

We're both wearing headsets and oxygen masks. The

headset so we can hear each other over the roar of the engine and the wind. The oxygen mask because—I don't know why, I just know that I would feel a lot safer in a plane where one wasn't required.

The turbulence up here is something else, and the rust bucket rattles and shakes and lurches painfully, setting my stomach lurching in response.

Which is why, although Sarroch is helpfully pointing out the world's tallest mountains as we pass them, I'm far too busy white-knuckling my armrests, gritting my teeth, and trying not to reach for my air sick bag.

The leather covering my seat is cracked and split, allowing the stuffing to show through, the padding so thin I can feel the seat's steel frame digging into my sit bones and back. Some kind of strap—maybe normally used to secure cargo?—dangles to the right of my head, hitting me in the temple every time the plane shakes. Which is often. The strap is worn ragged in places, like everything in this damn death trap.

Why I agreed to climb aboard a plane that's held together by optimism and prayer, I don't know. Must have been a moment of temporary insanity. A moment of temporary insanity that might well result in my untimely death.

My breathing is heaving in and out of my nose like I'm a panicked cow on the way to the slaughterhouse, and my mouth is filled with the bitter tang of panic. In short, this flight is bloody miserable.

"Apiya, if you open your eyes, you can see Everest over there." Sarroch's voice is irritatingly cheerful in my headset.

I foolishly—stupidly, moronically, and every kind of synonym for total bloody idiot you can think of—open my eyes. Yes, that is Everest, a little below us, ahead to the left.

Everest. The tallest mountain in the world. Thirty thousand feet of inhospitable snow and ice-covered rock.

And we're above it in a rust bucket that can barely keep itself together.

The plane bucks as if attempting to throw us out, and then gives a long, drawn out shiver that sets everything—including my teeth—rattling loudly, as the turbulence toys with us.

I close my eyes again. Sarroch has strong abilities with metal, but are they strong enough to prevent a rust bucket from plummeting out of the sky and crashing to the ground? If we crash here, no one will find the plane. And if the crash doesn't kill us, the cold will.

As if hearing my thoughts, the plane gives an almighty lurch and then abruptly drops out of the sky. Not low enough that we're in danger of crashing into the mountains, but enough that all my organs leap up and cram themselves into my throat as I scream in fear, clinging to my armrests so hard my hands hurt.

"Ohmygod, ohmygod, *ohmygod*!!!"

"It's fine, Apiya. Really. Trust me, I'm a good pilot. And if all else fails I can keep the plane flying using magic."

I don't open my eyes again. "Your qualities as a pilot are not in question," I tell him through clenched teeth. "The ability of this *damn plane* to remain whole and in the air *is*."

"It's a bit old and worn, I'll grant you, but it's still perfectly serviceable."

The plane rattles again, hard enough that it feels like it's trying to take itself apart in midair.

"This plane is as serviceable for flying as a geriatric with a zimmer frame is suitable for the gymnastic Olympics!" I snap.

Sarroch laughs.

I could kill him. If we survive this flight, I might just do that. What is wrong with him that this is the most relaxed he's been since my trial? Well, more to the point, since we've found ourselves needing to hot-wire a mating bond between us when his tiger doesn't want me.

If we don't manage to make that happen, my head goes straight back on the chopping block because the Mayak defence laws won't apply to me, and I killed another Mayak. It was self-defence, but apparently they only apply that important aspect of their laws to other Mayaks, not to humans.

Which is why I need to become Sarroch's mate, so I can be recognised as a Mayak and have the self-defence clause apply to me. Sarroch hasn't been mad keen on the idea, mostly because his tiger not only doesn't want me as a mate, but seems to actively dislike me. The whole situation is a bit of a disaster, so Sarroch has been understandably a little tense.

That is, until we stepped into this death-trap of an excuse for a plane. Apparently, near-death experiences relax him. Who knew? Certainly not me, for the very simple reason that no sane person would willingly put themselves through this. Yes, I am questioning Sarroch's sanity right now.

By some miracle, we continue on our journey without dropping from the sky, crashing, and without the plane spontaneously disintegrating. The turbulence finally reduces to a more manageable level, so the plane only shakes and trembles periodically, and I reopen my eyes.

The snowy peaks of the top of the Himalayas have made way for lower, brown and green mountains

"Okay, we're going to start our descent," Sarroch announces cheerfully. "Your trial is almost over."

"Stop being so bloody perky."

I can tell he's grinning at me from the way his eyes crinkle above his oxygen mask.

Now, normally I really like his smile. Sarroch is definitely one of life's more serious men, all capable, efficient, and aloof, but when he smiles, it gives him a boyish quality, warming his face and making his eyes dance. Normally, when said smile is directed at me, my stomach tends to do a happy little flip.

However, right now my stomach is still lodged in my throat along with my heart, kidneys, intestines, and all the rest of my innards, so nothing in my guts is in the mood to do a happy flip.

"Come on, Apiya, it really isn't that bad."

"I like being alive, Sarroch, and do you know what I enjoy even more than just being alive? Being alive without continually feeling like any moment I might be off to meet my maker."

"I'm sure Qinglong would be delighted to get some more time with you." He winks.

Murder. Cold bloody murder if he keeps that up—I'm not kidding. I take a deep, calming breath before I actually follow through on my murderous thoughts. I need him to land the plane, after all.

On the plus side, if the rust bucket managed to pass the Himalayas, then we should now be fine. The hardest part of the journey will have been flying over the roof of the world, right? So it should be all easy peasy going forward.

That is, until I remember what our destination is.

Paro, Bhutan. I foolishly looked it up before leaving. Google helpfully informed me that it is one of the top ten most dangerous airports to land at. A fact I *wish* I didn't know right now.

It hadn't seemed so bad finding that out when I still entertained the delusion that I would be making the landing in something modern. Something with lots of reassuring, glowing digital screens, automatic systems, and other bits of high tech that keep the plane purring along.

The rust bucket's cockpit doesn't have a single digital anything—instead there are lots of little dials with needles indicating...things. Whatever these things are. Sarroch seems to be able to make sense of them, which is slightly reassuring. Less reassuring is the fact that more than one of these dials has a cracked glass covering. Do they still work if the glass is broken?

That's anyone's guess. I'm praying they do, just like I'm praying the plane doesn't disintegrate during the landing manoeuvre.

Google's helpful article on the world's most dangerous airports also informed me that only two dozen pilots are actually licensed to make the landing at Paro Airport. I asked Sarroch if he was licensed before we headed to the plane. He thought it was a funny question and told me that he has flown in and out of Paro enough times. Not exactly the answer I wanted, but at the time, I had taken that as him being self-deprecating or modest. Given that he thinks this plane is serviceable, I'm now seriously questioning the soundness of his judgement.

And just like that, my nerves spike again at the thought of the landing ahead.

Sarroch goes through a short checklist, reading each item aloud and confirming their status. And then he says four words that send pure terror plummeting into my poor, already tortured stomach.

"Turning GPWS system off." And he flips a switch.

"What?" I squeak. "Isn't that something you need? Isn't

GPS or GPWs, whatever that is, pretty important when landing at one of the world's most dangerous airports? Turn it back on!"

"No need. There's no radar. We have to do the landing manually, by eye."

"What?" My voice has grown so shrill I'm pretty sure human ears would struggle to hear me. Good thing Sarroch's a weretiger. "That's...that's crazy," I squeak, my breath once again heaving through my nose.

"It'll be fine. Don't worry."

The plane rattles and lurches. I cling to my armrest as my stomach lurches painfully in response. "Oh god. Oh *god*."

"The turbulence is quite bad today," Sarroch comments mildly, in the tone of one remarking on a gentle breeze.

Did I mention the murderous thoughts earlier?

The turbulence *is* bad, *and* we have to land without radar. I think I'm in danger of crushing my armrests. I'm not ready to die. I'm *so* not ready to die.

The plane starts to lower, but we're still facing mountains, rather than the kind of nice *flat* expanse of land I've come to associate with airports. And more to the point, I don't see any cities on the horizon. Nothing but rocky terrain, the kind that isn't forgiving if a plane goes crashing into it.

"Um, Sarroch, where is Paro?" I'm not even trying to keep the panic from my voice.

"We won't actually see it for a little while. It's behind those mountains over there. We have to lower into the valley, and then bank left, keeping to a forty-five degree angle. The reason this landing is tricky is that we won't actually see the airfield until the last moment. So we have to get the plane in alignment without actually *seeing* the landing strip."

And without radar. I feel nauseous. "Jesus, Mary, Joseph, and a bloody camel."

"You're probably better off invoking Buddha here, since it's a Buddhist country." I hate how much Sarroch is enjoying this.

"Stop making stupid comments and focus on the damn mountains." I'll admit I'm starting to feel a tad hysterical. I'm not such a bad flyer normally, but I swear, this would test the most hardened traveller.

We continue to drop altitude, the rust bucket rattling harder, occasionally lurching like a horse at a rodeo. I can make out neat squares of rice paddies down in the narrow valley below and buildings on the foothills climbing up on either side of us.

Still no sign of an airstrip. And the valley is so narrow. Dangerously narrow. Sarroch manoeuvres the plane, and we bank left, the plane remaining tilted.

We're getting seriously close to the ground now. If it wasn't for the fear roiling in my belly, I would be quite fascinated by the beautiful Bhutanese buildings. But they're far too close to the plane's wings for comfort.

And then finally, I spot the airstrip, like an oasis after a long trek through the desert.

The landing is much like the entire flight—painful, jerky, death-defying.

The plane bounces a couple of times, the roar of the engine becoming painfully loud, while the plane makes a final, last-ditch effort to disintegrate on the runway.

By some miracle, the prayers and optimism work, holding it in one piece. It comes to a stop *before* the end of the runway, *and* without torrents of smoke pouring out of the engine.

The propeller has slowed right down, and Sarroch manoeuvres us off the runway.

He removes his oxygen mask and smiles at me. "Welcome to Bhutan." He leans over towards me, pulling the headset off my ears and releasing my oxygen mask. "Those were some highly entertaining squeals at the end." He laughs, straightening up. "And that is cold murder in your eyes or I'm not a weretiger."

Correct.

2

I 've always thought of airports as being uniform. At best, inoffensive steel and glass buildings, at worst concrete monstrosities—and never something I have an interest in.

Well, Paro Airport might well be the only exception to that. The terminal building is actually beautiful. Not beautiful just for an airport. *Actually* beautiful.

It's a traditional Bhutanese style building, and as my first introduction to the country's architecture, it's a mighty fine representation.

A slightly slanted, multi-tiered green roof overhangs richly decorated walls. Long rows of windows look over the airstrip, each window framed in painted wood with red and white patterns. The lower half of the wall is pristine white, without any dust or mud marring the surface. And you know what a sucker I am for a clean surface.

The shape of the building itself is quite heavy and square, but somehow, maybe because of how beautiful the walls are, it doesn't look squat. In fact, it's so gorgeous and otherworldly that it makes for a jarring contrast to the mobile stairways and other bits of modern equipment parked in front of it. Behind it, the mountains rise up, rugged and majestic, now that I'm able to safely admire them from ground level.

"Wow," I whisper, leaning a little forward and staring out of the cockpit.

It's almost enough to make me forget the ordeal of the journey. Almost.

With efficient gestures, Sarroch unstraps himself and helps me to get out of my own seat. I groan as I stand up, blood rushing back to my legs—with all the trauma, I hadn't noticed that the uncomfortable seat had basically cut off circulation to my lower limbs.

"Are you okay to walk?" Sarroch asks me, frowning with concern. A valid question since I have to prop myself up with one hand on the back of my seat to stop the dizziness. "Would you like me to carry your bag?"

I shake my head. "I got it. I just stood up a bit too fast, that's all."

His face relaxes again into a smile tinged with apology. "I didn't realise you were such a nervous flyer."

"I'm not a nervous flyer," I protest. "Put me in a Boeing and I'm good as gold. This, however..." I gesture at the rust bucket.

Sarroch pats the plane's wall. The plane's fuselage? I don't know what you call the parts of a plane, and after today I don't ever care to know.

"I, for one, rarely feel as alive as I do when flying," he says.

"Well, I'm glad at least one of us enjoyed the experience."

The dizziness has cleared, and I grab my backpack before eagerly following Sarroch out of the plane and onto the blessedly solid tarmac. I now understand why sometimes in movies people kneel down and kiss the ground. Doing so right now would barely be over the top.

The air is fresh up here and it smells clean and sharp, the wind tugging playfully at my pink hair. Airports are normally noisy, with planes taking off or landing, and various support vehicles beeping as they trundle along the airstrip.

Now that the rust bucket has stopped, there isn't any noise in Paro Airport. Like *nothing*. We could be on the side of a mountain—well, we *are* on the side of a mountain—and other than the wind and some birds in the distance, all is quiet. Not a single other plane is in operation.

Two men are waiting for us by the airport entrance—an entrance that is framed by an impressive carved wooden porch, supported by thick columns. The men are wearing what I assume must be traditional Bhutanese dress. Long-sleeved, knee-length robes that wrap around their bodies and are kept in place by a belt at their hips. The cuffs of the sleeves are white and large enough to come halfway up their forearms, a bright contrast to the dark red and orange patterned fabric of the rest of the robes.

It goes without saying that the white of the cuffs is as pristine as the walls of the airport. I already like Bhutan.

Beneath the robes, the men both wear knee-high black socks and brown leather shoes. The robes' patterns are different—one man wears stripes, while the other has a pretty mix of checks and circular patterns.

The two men and Sarroch seem to know each other, exchanging bows and greetings in Bhutanese. I can't tell whether Sarroch is fluent, but it's clear that he's able to converse very well.

"Welcome to Bhutan," one of the men says to me in heavily accented English.

"Thank you."

"Did you have a good flight?"

Answering no would be rude, so I make a noncommittal noise. Next to me, Sarroch snorts in amusement, his eyes gleaming mischievously as they catch mine. He really *is* in a good mood. It's contagious, and I find myself smiling in response.

The two men usher us into the airport. The inside of the building is as beautiful and heavily patterned as the outside, the walls decorated with lovely tiles. The floor is so clean, you could eat off it. That goes a long way towards soothing my frazzled nerves, and I find myself relaxing for the first time since I set foot in the rust bucket.

Oh yes, I have a feeling that I'm going to enjoy Bhutan.

Sarroch and the two men continue to talk, and I hang back, grateful to have a quiet moment to myself. Since there are no other planes in operation, the airport is completely empty. The only sound is the men's voices up ahead and our footsteps on the tiles.

In short, a world away from the usual chaos of airport arrivals. *This* kind of travel I could get used to, if only it didn't require a dance with death to get here.

I duck into a bathroom (do I need to comment on how impeccably clean it is?) to splash water on my face and brush my teeth in an attempt to wash the horror of the flight away, and by the time I rejoin Sarroch and the others I'm feeling pretty much back to myself.

It's not until we step out of the building that I realise we haven't gone through immigration.

"Wait, doesn't anyone need to see our passports?"

Sarroch shakes his head. "I already sent ahead all the information they would need. It's fine."

One of the men slips his hand inside the cross-body opening of his robe and pulls out an envelope and a set of keys.

Sarroch takes them both with a formal bow of thanks. And then the two men head back inside the building.

I look back after them, bewildered. "Is that really all? No security, no passport check? Don't they need to check whether I'm smuggling drugs in my backpack?"

Sarroch raises an eyebrow. "Are you smuggling drugs in your backpack?"

"Only if you consider the toothpaste that fuels my addiction to clean teeth to be a drug."

Sarroch laughs at that.

"No, but seriously, shouldn't there be more checks? Also, I read online that open tourism isn't allowed in Bhutan, and that any foreigner had to be accompanied by an official guide. Is this special treatment because you're a hotshot CEO or something?"

"Ah, but we're not tourists. Nor are we a regular arrival. The werecat community has a special place here, and over time we've been able to make certain...arrangements."

"You mean some of the Mayak are out in the open in Bhutan?"

"Not quite. It's more selective than that. But yes, a few Bhutanese Mundanes are aware of us, and they work with us to keep things...smooth and uncomplicated."

Interesting.

"Normally a Mundane plane would have to register its arrival seven days ahead," Sarroch continues, "and there's a lot of paperwork to go through. I can organise last minute arrivals if it's important, which this is."

The airport car park is almost as empty as the airport itself, and we slip into an old but well-maintained car. In fact, a car that inspires a heck of a lot more confidence than Sarroch's so-called plane.

As he starts the car, I find myself grateful that he's a more careful plane pilot than a car driver, because he sends the car shooting forward in a screech of tyres against the tarmac. If he'd flown the plane like that, I don't know if I'd have survived the ordeal.

3

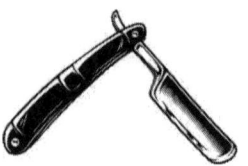

At first we drive in silence, largely because I'm too busy looking out the window. The scenery is stunning, the mountains majestic and covered in lush forest that stretches for miles in every direction. There's a feeling of primal, untouched nature. Of huge open spaces. Something you rarely see any more in this modern, developed world.

My mum would love it here.

"We'll pass through Park City," Sarroch tells me.

"That's not the capital, right?"

"Right. The capital is Thimphu. We've got about a half an hour drive to get to our destination."

"Which is?"

"The Tiger's Nest Monastery."

"No stopover in a hotel?"

"Nope. Straight to business, meaning to the werecat realm. We don't really have the luxury of time." In spite of the implications of what he's saying, he looks relaxed, with a ghost of a smile on his face.

"You're enjoying this, aren't you?"

He grins, never taking his eyes off the road. "I suppose I am." He's holding the steering wheel with one hand, the other on the gearshift. There's something seriously attractive about a man who can handle himself in a motorised vehicle. Other than a plane.

His window is lowered, the wind mussing his hair. With the stubble on his jaw, he looks younger and more rugged than when he's wearing his expensive suits. Today he's got on a black t-shirt and khaki, military style trousers tucked into black lace up military boots.

Have I mentioned that he looks amazing with stubble? I probably have. Still, it's worth reiterating. He really does. And now that I'm not clinging on for dear life, my stomach is free to do that happy flip at seeing him smile.

It's also a nice change. This is a world away from how tense and unhappy he was with the situation back in Panong. He really wasn't happy with me claiming him as mate in front of all the Elders, and to be fair, I did put him on the spot.

But seeing him looking so relaxed now has me thinking that maybe he's not quite so unhappy with the situation as he made out back in Panong.

"What are you enjoying exactly?" I ask him. "I mean, our situation hasn't changed since we left Panong..."

"I know I just...I don't know. I feel lighter for some reason. Flying always helps with that. And I think I'm looking forward to showing you the weretiger realm."

The Tiger's Nest Monastery, or Taktsang, isn't only the most holy site of Bhutan, it's also the doorway to the were-cat's realm. As Sarroch explained before we left, they have a number of different realms, including one in Panong, but this is their stronghold. Their HQ.

I smile, looking back out of the window—the scenery

whizzing past is just gorgeous. Rugged and mountainous and wild. Sarroch's good mood is contagious, and for a moment, I can kid myself that we truly are just on a road trip. "I thought it was a realm for all werecats, not just weretigers," I tease.

"Well...I won't go as far as to say the others are less significant, but..."

I laugh. "That's exactly what you're saying."

"They'd say the same about me," he replies casually.

"Do you all get along well?" I ask, curious.

"Sure. We have strict rules and no one breaks them because of the resulting loss of face."

We continue driving in silence, while I enjoy the view.

"We're approaching Paro," Sarroch announces. I perk up, curious as to what a city will look like in a country that makes such beautiful airports.

I'm pretty sure Paro is supposed to be a big city by Bhutanese standards, but I would easily have mistaken it for a small town. I've never seen a city that looks so peaceful. Especially not in Asia. Big cities in Asia are fast and loud, a real assault on the senses. Go to Jakarta, Bangkok, Hong Kong, it's all the same: an overload of sights and sounds and smells, among a rush of movement.

Not so in Paro. It's not quite like we've gone back in time. There are cars and people wearing 'modern' clothing— although a lot are wearing traditional Bhutanese dress, like the men who waited for us at the airport.

But there are no traffic lights and no billboards. In fact, other than lovely, often hand-painted signs atop shop door-ways, there is no advertising of any kind. And while there are cars, very few of them are on the road.

People walk the streets looking cheerful and unhurried. Said streets are lined with beautiful buildings, like the one at the airport. Square bases with slightly angled roofs, and each one has beautifully decorated walls and rows of windows encased in carved or painted wooden frames. Each building is different from the next, displaying both the care and creativity the Bhutanese clearly take with construction. And of course it helps that the town is framed by those beautiful mountains.

As we continue down the quiet streets, the feeling that the rest of the world is locked far, far away increases. There's no McDonalds. No ads for Coca Cola. No 7-11 convenience stores. No ugly neon, no cheap posters. Everything is done and built with careful attention.

I *love* it. And I really wish I could spend time exploring this lovely little town. Or city. Whatever it is. I want to get to know it better, get to know its people, visit its monuments, and get to grips with its culture. Even passing through, tucked away behind a car window, I can sense all the care that has gone into every aspect of this town, and it resonates deeply within me, tugging at a harp string within my soul. If I wasn't born in Panong, I'd say that in Bhutan I've found my people.

"Have you spent much time in Bhutan?" I ask Sarroch, still glued to my window, nearly pressing my nose against the glass like a child.

Sarroch nods. "I have spent quite a bit of time here, over the centuries. It's a very special place. We're lucky the Bhutanese Mundanes have been smart enough to keep it out of the world's spotlight." His voice turns bitter. "Like Panong was, before the recent developments..."

I turn to look at him. "Sarroch Industries is a big part of those developments..."

"When change comes, there are two options. The first is to let the wave of change drown you. The second is to surf the wave, to get involved and be a part of it so you can keep some control, maybe even shape the changes. I chose the latter."

That makes a lot of sense.

As we reach the end of Paro and head up into the mountains, I can't help a twang of disappointment. The mountains are beautiful, sure, but I still feel the tug to return to Paro. Maybe we can come back once our business with the werecats is completed.

The Mayak Elders gave us until the next full moon to have a mating bond in place, and that is just a few days away. As we climb up a steep road, the reality of why we're here starts to sink in again, and all the cheer from earlier evaporates. I hope Sarroch's optimism that we can get help here is warranted. I really don't have it in me to face down the Mayak Elders again.

4

I didn't just Google the airport before getting on the plane—I also looked into the Tiger's Nest Monastery to try to assuage some of my curiosity. The monastery is halfway up a mountain, clinging to a sheer rocky cliff. The only way to get to it is by hiking, which according to a blog post I read should take about three or four hours, fitness depending.

Which is why as Sarroch brings the car to a stop, I'm expecting us to be at the official start of the trail, where stalls sell things like hiking sticks, water, and where people offer the possibility of doing part of the trail on the back of a mule. There should also be a number of other tourists, as this is *the* big item everyone wants to visit when they come to Bhutan.

Instead, we've stopped at a completely deserted spot without so much as a post to mark the start of the trail. Sarroch gets out of the car.

"Not taking it all the way to the top?" I ask him with a raised eyebrow.

He shakes his head. "That would be disrespectful in the extreme."

"Why would it be so much more disrespectful than what you did back in Panong?"

"That entrance in Panong is one of the lesser used entrances—a back door, if you will—to Mucalinda's private residence. This is the main entrance to the werecat's stronghold, and it also happens to be the Bhutanese Mundanes' most holy site. We have a good relationship with the Mundanes who know about us, and I don't want to jeopardise that. And while time is of the essence, a couple of hours won't make much of a difference, unlike the situation with Mucalinda."

I nod. Makes sense. "Okay, well let me get my backpack from the boot and I'm ready to go."

"I told you, you'll have everything you need once we get there."

"That's as may be, but there are certain things I want to have with me." Like my toothbrush and deodorant, because I don't know whether the Mayak use either of those things. I'm not precious, but basic hygiene isn't something I'm prepared to do without.

With that in mind, I also have a change of clothes packed, and since I've learnt my lesson from my time in the baku realm, I also have a bunch of cutthroat razors with me, including one magical one, and one silver one. Just to be safe. My backpack, in short, should ensure I stay clean and alive for however long we're up there.

Sarroch locks the car, and we start up the trail. I've come prepared for the trek, with high black hiking boots, leggings, and a couple of layers so I can either strip down to my racer back top or cover up with a hoodie and fleece if it gets cold.

Given the steepness of the trail and the speed at which

Sarroch walks, I quickly stuff my hoodie in my backpack to keep my arms bare.

The trees stretch high overhead, the trail zigzagging between them. Here and there, colourful prayer flags flutter in the wind, tied up to tree trunks. The air is sharp with the smell of resin from the conifers we pass, the crunch of pine needles beneath our feet the only sound other than the bright scraps of fabric flapping in the wind.

"We'll be arriving from the back," Sarroch informs me.

"From the back?" I've seen pictures of the Tiger's Nest Monastery, but just to be sure my memory isn't playing tricks on me, I pull out my phone and check the pictures I've saved. The monastery hangs off sheer cliffs, and even from the photos, it's very obvious that there is only one entrance —at the front, where the main trail leads. The back is all sheer rock.

I scamper forward to catch up to Sarroch and show him my phone screen. "Unless those pictures are incorrect, what you just said means we will either rock climb up, or abseil down to the monastery."

Sarroch grins at me. "I didn't picture you as a worrier, Apiya. You're worrying a lot on this trip."

"Yeah, well, recent events have given me cause. So? How are we getting to the Tiger's Nest?"

"You'll see."

Sarroch continues on, and I hurry to stay level with him. His legs are long, taking powerful strides. I'm not quite trotting to keep up, but not far off.

"Is there even an entrance at the back?" I ask him.

"You'll see." Now he looks downright amused.

"Sarroch, withholding information from me is how we ended up in this mess in the first place, remember?"

"In this instance, nothing can go wrong. It's all pretty straightforward."

"I wouldn't be so sure," I mutter. One thing's become abundantly clear these last few months: my ability to get myself in trouble far outweighs my ability to get myself out of it. Which isn't a good combination.

We continue up the trail. It's steep, but the scenery is breathtaking, with stunning views of the mountains.

"Is the legend true?" I asked Sarroch. "About the buddhist master who came here on the back of a flying tigress? The story goes that he meditated in some caves in the mountain, which then became what is now the Tiger's Nest Monastery." That little nugget of information came from my father. Some people wish their children a safe flight. My father disgorges a quantity of facts any time I'm about to travel somewhere. It has its uses.

"I wasn't flying," Sarroch replies casually. "And I'm very much male. Mundanes have a hard time getting Mayak genders right in their stories."

I laugh. "Seriously?"

"Seriously. I did make the winds cooperate with us, though, to help at the end, but most of the journey was done by foot. And it goes without saying that he *never* rode on my back." His tone of voice is pure feline—contempt that borders on disgust at the thought of someone riding him.

Which to be fair is a lot more realistic than a tigress allowing a Mundane to ride on her back. Even a super zen, totally enlightened Buddhist master.

5

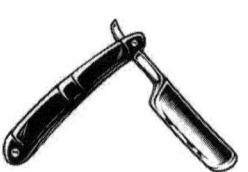

After a while, the trail becomes significantly more steep, and given the punishing pace that Sarroch is setting, I fall silent to concentrate on my breathing and aching legs. I haven't been working out these last few weeks, what with being stuck at home, and I can really feel the drop in my fitness levels. Doing a challenging hike so soon after feeling so miserably queasy on the plane doesn't help, either.

The world falls away, narrowing to nothing more than the next step, and then the next. I soon have to clamber over rocks using my hands when the trail grows too steep, and my quads are burning from the effort of hauling my weight up.

The difficulty of the trek is offset by the fact that since I'm lagging behind, I get a good view of Sarroch's bum. And yes, it looks mighty fine in those khaki military style trousers. They suit him, as does the black t-shirt. Although to be fair, everything suits him.

Silver linings and all that.

Of course, he's not even out of breath, and I've yet to see

him break into sweat. I, on the other hand, am breathing as hard as a smith's forge, and from the heat in my face, I must be approaching the colour of a tomato. Which is unfortunate when you have pink hair. Definitely not in my most seductive 'take-me-as-your-mate' mode.

"We're at the halfway point," Sarroch suddenly says, stopping abruptly.

I stop and look up, relieved for the break. There's a huge prayer wheel up ahead, sheltered beneath a small roof supported on four pillars. Kind of like a Panongian beruga without a floor. I have no idea what the Bhutanese call that kind of thing.

The prayer wheel is painted with a mantra written on it. The floorless beruga is also painted, so that the whole thing looks colourful and happy, popping out from the backdrop of dark trees and grey rock. More prayer flags have been tied from the pillars to the neighbouring trees, and they all flutter happily on the wind.

Buddhists believe that by spinning a prayer wheel, the prayers painted or carved onto them are sent out into the world, and it allows the person who spun the wheel to earn good karma. I'd go spin the wheel, but I'm tired and I've scuffed a bit of skin off the heel of my right hand clambering over some of the rocks. Karma will have to wait—this gal needs some R&R.

We sit by the prayer wheel for a moment, catching our breath. When I say 'our', I'm obviously using the royal we because Sarroch is as fresh as if he'd just been strolling around Old Town.

"You like to climb fast," I comment, gulping down some water from the bottle I was smart enough to bring with me from Panong. When Sarroch told me there would be everything I need at the werecat's realm, he obviously forgot that a human would need water on the way over.

"Oh. Am I going too fast?" Sarroch's expression turns apologetic. "Maybe you should go ahead for the rest of it, set a pace that suits you better."

"I'm fine with you staying ahead. Just remember to check on me from time to time, and bear in mind that while Qinglong made me, my body is very much human, with human limitations. But it's been quite a long time since I've had some proper exercise with all this being stuck at home business, so I'm enjoying the challenge."

Plus, if I go ahead, I'll lose my view of his bum. A thought I keep to myself.

My stomach rumbles, and I pull out a granola bar, another thing I now congratulate myself for having had the foresight to pack. Clever me. I grab another one and gesture it at him. "Want some?"

He grimaces, looking downright embarrassed. "I forgot you'd need food and water for this part. Sorry, Apiya. I haven't done this trek with a human since... Well since that Buddhist master. And even then we went a different, easier way—the way that leads to the front of the monastery."

"Not to worry. It's why I make it a policy not to listen to you when you're wrong." I smile sweetly at him.

He laughs easily. I'm liking this new relaxed relationship we've slipped into. Hopefully, it's a sign that things will go well once we reach the werecat realm, although I don't bank on it. That's something else I've recently learnt—if things can become complicated or difficult, or if they can get royally screwed, they inevitably will. Call it Apiya's law.

I carefully stash the granola bar wrapper back in my backpack—my childhood was peppered by lectures from my mother on the principles of Leave No Trace—and we head off again.

We pass a waterfall at the foot of which is a statue that's covered in slick green moss—or maybe it's algae. I'm too far away to see. The statue is half hidden by the shade and spray from the waterfall, so I can't see it very well, but something about it gives me a shiver of intuition.

"What's that?" I ask Sarroch, pointing at the statue.

"Well spotted. That's the entrance to another Mayak realm, although nothing that concerns us for today."

"Another one? Are there a lot of Mayak realms here?"

"A few. Not as many as in Panong."

"This one gives me a bad vibe."

"That'll be because your body is recognising the lair of a predator whose diet is mostly humans..."

I shudder and trot quickly after Sarroch, staying very close. Looking around me at the wilderness, though, and thinking back to Paro with its lack of modern buildings and traffic, with its slow and relaxed pace, this seems like a far more suitable place for the Mayak to establish themselves than Panong.

I tell Sarroch as much.

"Yes, it seems that, with hindsight, we picked wrong when we chose Panong as our capital. At the time, Panong was such a small, backwater place, especially since it's an island, we never imagined it would change as much as it did. And Bhutan borders India, which was developing scarily fast due to the British presence there at the time. We thought Bhutan would follow suit. We were wrong."

"Then why don't you all move? Wouldn't coming here resolve a lot of the problems the Mayak have with the Mundanes?"

Sarroch shook his head. "That comes with its own set of

problems. There's the fact that we are now so heavily established in Panong that such a move, given all the various
spaces and realms we have created there, would be very
long and complicated. And more importantly, such a move
would be akin to admitting defeat. It would mean that
neither war nor peaceful cohabitation is possible. Or that
we attempted war and lost and had to retreat. There's far too
much pride involved for this to be a solution anyone would
be willing to consider."

The Mayak and their pride. It's one of those bottomless
things, like the self-deprecation of the British. "I kinda get it,
but if you ask me, it's stupid to let something like pride get
in the way, when there could be so many advantages to
coming out here. Say for the pari-pari. The wilderness here
might make it easier for them to hatch younglings."

"The pari-pari are the least likely among us to leave.
They become part of the environment they live in, in a way
most of us never fully achieve. Things would have to be
truly dire and desperate to force them to leave, and even
then it would probably only happen with the wholesale
destruction of Panong's forest."

I shiver at the thought. That is, of course, the way a lot of
places in South East Asia go—forests are cut down to make
way for palm oil plantations to supply the big processed
food companies that feed the Western world. I was never
allowed Nutella as a kid for that very reason. Nor was I
allowed any of the usual sugary, processed treats that kids
love, instead receiving detailed lectures about the damage
the processed food companies do to the environment.

I really, really hope Panong never falls prey to the palm
oil industry.

"Come on, let's continue." Sarroch heads off once again.

He's still walking at a very decent pace, but he's making

an obvious effort to slow down to something a little more accessible for me, which I'm grateful for. We're high up, the air is thin, which is probably why I'm huffing and puffing far more than I would normally. Nothing to do with my fitness having fallen by the wayside of late, of course...

All thoughts leave my head when we turn a bend and the view opens up, giving us our first sighting of the Tiger's Nest Monastery.

I gasp, delighted. It's one thing to see it in photos, but seeing it in the flesh is something else entirely.

The monastery is built in that same Bhutanese style as the other buildings, with a heavy, square base of white walls that are decorated at the top. The roofs are red and gold, only slightly slanted.

But the most incredible thing is how large the network of buildings is, given the tiny amount of space they're built on. The edge of the outer walls of the monastery are flush with the mountainside, the walls looking like they are rising from the rock itself. The other side of the monastery presses up against the rock as it rises high and sheer overhead, seeming to meld into it.

The buildings are set up in a line, with the largest in the middle of the narrow platform.

We've actually climbed a little higher than the Monastery, and as Sarroch predicted, we're at the back of it. I can just about make out movements on the other side—no doubt tourists and pilgrims coming and going.

And more importantly, as far as I can see, there is absolutely no way to get from where we are to where the monastery is.

"So what now?" I ask.

"Now you have to trust me."

"What does that mean, exactly?" I ask suspiciously.

"It means we'll have to jump, but I'll get us there."

My jaw does a credible attempt at dropping to the ground.

"Jump? Here?" I squeak. "It's impossibly far to the monastery and there's nothing but rocks to land on very, very far below. You might be made of magic, but I'm not."

"I have my ways with the wind. We should make it fine."

"Should? *Should* is nowhere near good enough." My voice is growing so high-pitched, I'm pretty sure if I keep going only dogs will be able to hear me.

Sarroch turns serious. "I was only kidding. We'll make it absolutely fine. I've done this thousands of times. There's really nothing for you to worry about."

"You told me you haven't done the hike with a human since the Buddhist master," I counter. This is not a time to overlook such a detail, not when a wrong move could mean my parents get notified that their daughter had to be scraped off the rocks at the bottom of a Bhutanese mountain.

"It will be fine—having you with me won't be a problem," Sarroch replies in a way I'm sure he means to be soothing. It fails in the face of the sheer, sheer rock. "You're so small and light, it won't be any different from when I'm alone."

I start to argue back. I have a few arguments, actually, which I pull out one after the other, throwing them at him as if they were playing cards, without waiting for him to reply. It's not until Sarroch grabs both my hands in his that I realise I'm babbling almost incoherently.

"Apiya," he says gently. "I think the last few days are catching up with you."

I fall silent. That's a pretty astute observation. There's been a lot of stress, a lot of fear, just a lot of overwhelm generally, ever since my trip to the baku realm, and there hasn't been much sleep. I'm not normally this wound up.

"It will be fine," Sarroch continues, his voice soft, as if he's trying to coax out a small animal from its burrow. "I know what I'm doing. I promise I will get you there safely. I swear, Apiya, no harm will come to you today. One final hurdle, and then we are in my kind's realm, and things will be better. Easier. You can rest, get some sleep, get some food..."

I take a deep breath. The thought of resting and food right now is music to my ears. "You promise you'll make sure I'm okay?" I glance once again at the vertiginous drop just beyond the edge of the rocky platform I'm standing on. I feel small and fragile, and suddenly very, very tired. It would be nice for things to go smoothly for once.

"I promise." He bends his head to catch my eyes. "I promise, Apiya. I *will* take care of you, and you *will* be fine."

I huff out a breath. What other option do I have but to trust him? The alternative is to return to Panong and face the music with the Mayak Elders. "All right. Okay. What do you need me to do?"

"Just hold on tight."

He slips a hand around my waist and pulls me close. His body feels hard and muscular, his arm reassuringly vice-like strong around me. He smells like leather and eucalyptus and soap, with something else beneath, something musky. It must be his tiger.

I'm suddenly reminded of the fact that if things go as I hope they will and we're able to finagle a mating bond, I'll be having sex with Sarroch at least once. Which...if I wasn't so tired, sweaty, and generally drained from our recent travels, I'd be feeling quite enthusiastic about.

"Ready?" he asks.

My heart starts to crash in my chest, and this time it has nothing to do with how Sarroch looks and everything to do with how the monastery gracefully hangs from the cliff.

The sheer, sheer, *stony* cliff.

I'm not ready. Not ready at all.

"Yes," I lie.

Sarroch jumps.

6

You know in those Indiana Jones movies, when Harrison Ford grabs the buxom blonde with one arm, his lasso in the other, and they swing together across the precipice, all smooth and cool, the buxom blond's legs bared to advantage as she gracefully holds onto his neck with a single, manicured hand?

Yeah, that is not how the jump with Sarroch goes.

When he jumps, for one terrifying, shit-my-pants moment, we drop like two stones. I scream so hard my voice breaks.

And then suddenly a gust of wind seems to lift us, tossing us forward like we're no more than two leaves.

I can feel the wind, the sudden weightlessness, but I can't look at what's going on. Maybe if I wasn't already traumatised by the ride in the rust bucket, I would have had the courage to open my eyes.

Instead, I continue screaming, my voice raw and broken, my eyes squeezed shut, as I cling to Sarroch and bury my face against his shoulder.

Which is why I don't actually realise when we've stopped moving.

"Apiya? Apiya. You can let go now."

I dare to squeeze an eye open.

Remember the buxom, leggy blonde I described earlier, she who holds onto Indiana Jones with one graceful hand? Now picture, if you will, a cross between a limpet and a baby monkey—with pink hair and tattoos. Not *quite* the same effect.

My arms and legs are wrapped tightly around Sarroch, so that even when he lets go of me, I'm still clinging to him, hovering a few feet off the ground.

Speaking of ground, he appears to be standing on something that looks solid. Something made of planks of wood, like a large platform. It's no longer daylight, but dusk, a deep, purply, warm dusk with shadows that feel welcomingly thick rather than creepy or threatening.

"So, finally you come to me," a voice says.

I disentangle myself from Sarroch to find a woman standing a couple of yards from us, watching us. Her skin is a couple of shades darker than mine, so that if she were human, she might look Northern Indian, Nepalese, or Bhutanese. I'm reaching for the Indian connection first on account of her clothes. A set of loose yellow trousers that gather at the ankles, a matching cropped top with short sleeves over which a sari is elegantly draped.

Her hair falls in twin, sleek grey waterfalls all the way to her waist, framing a face which is completely unlined, a sharp contrast with her hair. Her body is lean and muscled, and even though she's not moving, there's a feeling of power to her that belies the youth of her features. Her eyes are dark and large, her nose hooked. She's not beautiful in the sense of her features being pretty or perfect, but she's striking, and I'd challenge anyone to not look at her twice if they met her in the street.

Her septum is pierced with a simple gold ring, but there's nothing simple about the rest of her jewellery. Her ears are covered by the most incredible ear cuffs of intricately worked gold that fan out at the lobe. A fringe of tiny gold chains tipped with little black onyx bells dangle from the bottom of the cuffs, and they make a delicate sound as they sway gently. A gossamer fine gold chain supports a single onyx teardrop at her forehead, so that it covers where her third eye would be.

"Hello Pragya," Sarroch says, his tone wary.

"And you must be Apiya," she says to me.

Being caught in her gaze is unsettling.

"I am indeed." I try to keep my own voice relaxed, which isn't easy given that I haven't even had the time to recover from the jump.

Pragya looks at me in silence for just long enough for it to become awkward. It takes a huge effort of will on my part not to fidget nervously or look away.

"Will you help us?" Sarroch asks.

She finally turns back to him. "I want to hear you say it. That you are coming to me. That you will allow me to examine you."

"I want no such thing," Sarroch replies crossly. "I want your help because Apiya and I need a mating bond—"

"Yes, I heard. That's why I'd need to examine you."

"There is nothing wrong with me," Sarroch snaps, his nostrils flaring with anger. "Haven't you caused enough damage? Telling your stories, making sure no one ever forgets what I did."

"I believe that when a monster lives in your midst, it is important to be both aware and wary."

"I'm not a monster!" Sarroch's voice comes out in a roar underlined by his tiger. His fists are clenched, his eyes turning to ice. He's actually shaking.

Pragya seems undeterred. "Prove it," she says softly. "Allow me to look at you."

Sarroch turns away, disgusted. "I'm not playing your games."

"Would anyone mind bringing me up to speed?" I ask.

Pragya raises an eyebrow. "Sarroch hasn't explained?" She glances back at him. "Not exactly fair to let her claim you as her mate when she doesn't know the full truth of who you are."

"She knows," Sarroch replies tightly. "I told her." I'm assuming he's referring to the time when his mate died and he snapped, destroying an entire civilisation in a few days before Mr Sangong got him back under control. It's no small thing, and I still struggle to reconcile the Sarroch I know with the man who did that.

He whirls back to face Pragya. "I have never lost control since then. Never. Not once. And yet you refuse to let me move on from what I did. I am *not* a monster, Pragya." His voice quavers just a little. He almost manages to hide it, but I can sense the hurt that lies just beneath the surface.

"You might not be, but something inside you is. And that kind of thing doesn't go away on its own. Just because you have kept control of yourself until now doesn't mean you won't lose it again." Pragya's voice turns cold. "And if Apiya is foolishly trying to bind herself to you, she should have a full understanding of what she's getting into. Not that she has much in the way of options." Pragya's gaze softens as she turns back to me. "For what it's worth, I didn't agree with the way things were handled at your reckoning. I don't think you should have to bind yourself to Sarroch just to be allowed to defend your life. Some of us already consider you to be a part of the Mayak, given how you were created."

"Oh..." I'm so taken aback that for a moment, I can't think of what to say. "Thank you. That...it actually means a lot." And it does.

"Chizu had no right to try to destroy you."

"No, she didn't," Sarroch replies tightly. "Nothing about any of this is fair. Apiya should have more options than to have to take me for her mate, but the Mayak Elders have forced us to this position, and I'm not going to stand idly by and let Apiya be executed for the crime of defending her own life while in the process of trying to help another Mayak. And *that* is why we're here today, Pragya. Not to play any of your games or have you examine me to try to prove your theory that I am part monster."

The older woman cocks her head. "Fine. You take part in a hunt—both of you. You do this without anything going wrong, and I'll see what I can do to help create either a real mating bond or something that will be close enough to appease the Elders."

Sarroch frowns. "What..."

"Those are my conditions and they're not up for debate. A hunt during which nothing goes wrong. You do that and I will help you. But if something *does* go wrong, you agree to let me look at you."

"What do you expect will go wrong?" I ask her. This isn't making me feel comfortable at all.

Pragya's eyes are huge and dark once again, and completely unreadable. "I'm not sure. But I think something *will* go wrong."

"No, it will *not*," Sarroch replies forcefully, stabbing an index in her direction. "You know what, I'll play your stupid game. If the hunt goes without a hitch, you will see to it that

the stories about me stop. And you will publicly acknowl-
edge that I am not a risk to anyone."

"Fine. I will agree to your terms."

"And I agree to yours," Sarroch replies.

"Er, what about me?" I pipe up. "Because right now I
don't agree to take part. I don't know what this hunt is, and I
fail to see how putting me in the middle of a group of werecats with their blood up during a hunt is a good idea. I like
being in one piece—that's why I'm here in the first place."

"Oh, on that front there's nothing to worry about,"
Pragya replies. "We don't hunt anything alive. It's a contest of
agility and speed. We aren't *werewolves*." That last word is
uttered with pure feline contempt. "We don't get into
feeding frenzies. Feeding is a private thing. The hunt is a
contest to see who can first catch a flying orb of light as it
darts through the forest."

"Okay, but I still don't see how I'll be able to take part in
a contest of agility and speed among werecats."

"You ride motorbikes don't you?" Pragya asks. "Sarroch
will be able to sort something out for you," she continues
before I can reply. "And since all is taken care of, I will see
you both at the hunt."

And that, apparently, is that.

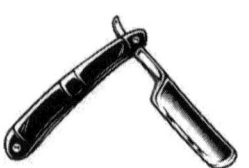

7

Sarroch leads the way across a bridge made of wood and knotted rope as we make our way to the rooms that have been put aside for us. Now that I'm free to look around, I can see just how breathtaking the realm of the werecats is.

It's like a whole city that has been built up in the trees, although the word 'tree' is hardly adequate to do justice to the behemoths stretching up around us. I've never seen trees like this before. If I glance down over the edge of the bridge, the ground isn't visible, disappearing into mist and darkness, but I can see enough to know that we are at vertiginous heights. The trunks are enormous, their circumference the size of a small house, their wood so smooth and sleek and dark, it looks like it has been varnished.

Branches stretch up overhead and below, some wide enough for two or even three people to walk abreast. The canopy of leaves is lush and thick, so much so that it's hard to know whether it truly is dusk or if we're just in a deep shadow.

Flowers bloom all over the trees, and they glow violet or

gold, depending on the tree, providing both light and a beautiful, otherworldly quality to the canopy. They also turn the gloom either a deep purple, the colour of dusk on a summer's night, or add a warm light, as if the sun is low on the horizon.

The perfume they give out is not unlike that of the frangipani I have in my courtyard, the smell comforting and familiar. The leaves themselves are of deep, dark green, tinged at the edges with blue. The trees near us have violet flowers, the muted light making the leaves look as soft and lush as velvet. The air is warm, far warmer than it was in Bhutan, but without being hot. The perfect temperature, in short.

Felines always know how to be comfortable, and it seems that werecats are no exception to that rule—they've made themselves a truly lovely place to live.

We reach the end of the bridge, stepping onto another wooden platform that's been built around a second, massive tree.

"We're going to the upper levels," Sarroch says.

A delicate, woven bamboo staircase winds up around the huge trunk.

"What do you think Pragya expects to happen during the hunt?" I ask him as we step up onto the stairs. The bamboo of the staircase is springy underfoot, and it creaks with each step.

"Probably something stupid like someone will jostle you, or put you in some kind of danger, and I'll snap."

"You sound like that's the most ridiculous thing ever. Can I just say that if I am in danger, I definitely would appreciate some kind of reaction from you. Preferably the kind of reaction that will ensure I'm no longer in danger."

"Of course I'd get involved. But I won't snap. I won't start destroying everything around me." His voice lowers to barely above a whisper. "I never have since then and never will again."

"If it helps at all, I believe you."

He stops and turns around on his step to look down at me. "Thank you Apiya. I'm not sure you can appreciate how much that means."

I shrug. "I don't believe in condemning a man for his past, and I like to judge people by the way they are acting right now."

We set off up the stairs again. I run a hand along the tree trunk that we're climbing up. Either it has no bark, or the bark is smooth as polished wood. I check quickly—the whole trunk looks that way, so it's not just a result of centuries of hands running against it around the staircase.

We pass one level and continue up to the next. On the way, we pass numerous structures nestled in the branches. Lower down they're made of wood, but higher above us they're made of woven bamboo and wicker, like giant baskets. The trees with the violet-glowing flowers are darker, and it's harder to make out the structures there, whereas further ahead I can see the trees with the gold flowers, and those are well lit.

People in human and cat form move about soundlessly, bare feet and paws making no noise against the wood and bamboo. What voices there are stay hushed, soft. No one shouts or calls, so instead the loudest sound is the trilling of birds higher up in the trees.

I'm amazed that there can be so many birds given all the werecats around, but I'm guessing the cats are all too big to be interested in prey as small as a bird. Either that or there aren't birds, and the sound is some kind of magic.

We reach the upper level, which is almost entirely made

of woven rope, bamboo, and wicker. Here the rooms are like woven wicker balls that hang from branches, swaying softly. The tree branches are narrower, although still easily thick enough to support a tiger or other large animal.

From our higher vantage point, I spot an area where the canopy is open and sunlight pours in. A great number of large cats are lounging in the sun, basking. Three tigers, some regular and snow leopards, two panthers, a lynx with those distinctively tufted ears, and some other large cats I can't identify.

They are all bigger than their regular, Mundane counterparts, with the sabre tooth-type canines that identify them as shifters. If I knew more about big cats, I could probably spot other differences compared to the Mundane species back in the human world.

One of the panthers gets up and heads over to a large post that has been erected to the side of the wooden platform. It looks like a giant version of a cat scratching post, and that is exactly what it is, the panther doing her claws on it with lazy movements before stretching luxuriously. She then selects another spot in the sun, lying gracefully back on the floor and yawning, displaying a shockingly pink tongue that stands out starkly against her black fur.

I can't help but smile. At the end of the day, werecats are clearly not that different from regular house cats... A thought I will be sure to keep to myself—I'm sure they wouldn't find the comparison flattering. I might tell Tim when I get back, though. I'm sure he'd probably deem them inferior to house cats, anyway.

A man walks past us, nodding a quick greeting at Sarroch. He's also dressed in loose cotton trousers, but his chest is bare, save for a large, carved piece of blue stone hanging on a leather thong.

Sarroch and I head over along a narrow walkway of woven bamboo. I'm grateful for the woven rope handrail, because one glance down is enough to establish that even if I just fell onto the lower levels, the distance would be enough to kill me.

A little girl who looks like she can't be more than six or seven comes pelting past us, chasing after what looks like a lynx cub. The girl is laughing, apparently not bothered by how narrow the walkway is, or by the fact that there are people already on it.

I cling to the handrail as I move to the side to let them pass, praying neither of them trips. But they're both so sure-footed, you'd think they were running on solid ground. Sarroch doesn't seem bothered or worried.

"All of our younglings are born and raised here," he says, as we set off again. "A necessity to ensure their safety after those clashes with the Mundanes that resulted in some of our young being killed. Ah, here we are," he says when we reach another platform.

8

W e're standing before a set of enormous, interconnected wicker baskets that hang from the branches overhead. Steps made of knotted rope lead up to the door.

"Those are the rooms we've been given for our stay," Sarroch says, stepping up to the door.

From the outside, the giant wicker structures look simple enough—just interconnected, woven globes without so much as a window to complicate the lines. Once we enter inside, however, the wicker is supported by a complex cross-hatching of long, curved bamboo poles. And the three inter-connecting globes are not, in fact, full globes at all. Instead, all three of them open up on the other side, facing a patch of canopy devoid of any other structures, so the view is completely private. The glowing flowers are violet, the gloom velvety.

The curves of the opening and of the bamboo give an elegant, sinuous feel to the rooms. Vines curl around the bamboo struts, and they produce golden, glowing flowers that are similar to those of some of the trees, bathing the rooms in soft light.

The central wicker globe is a lounge or living room of sorts, with furniture following soft organic shapes, also made of curved bamboo. A multitude of brightly coloured throw pillows makes the various seating options look inviting and comfortable.

To the right, an arched opening leads through to the next wicker globe—the bedroom. A second, smaller half globe, this one made of white cotton rather than wicker, houses the bed inside the bedroom. White curtains are tied to the sides of the cotton globe with white and gold ropes—I'm guessing when released, they provide a complete screen for privacy.

Speaking of privacy... To the left of the living area is the bathroom, but instead of a door there's just a colourful curtain of green and gold, with an embroidered pattern that matches the vines on the ceiling.

It's exceedingly pretty, don't get me wrong. However, I'm the kind of gal that normally prefers something a little bit more solid between myself and the world when I'm in the bathroom... Sarroch and I aren't really at the point where I'd feel comfortable with him hearing me pee. So that means I'll have to get creative when arranging to go to the bathroom.

And of course, it hasn't escaped my notice that there is only the one double bed. Which makes sense, given that Sarroch and I are supposed to be here to officialise our mating bond, but it also makes my heartbeat quicken.

"Okay, so take all the time you need if you want to rest before the hunt. Do you need anything to eat or drink?"

"Some water would be good." My stomach feels far too

knotted up for food. It needs some time to get over the flight, the jump, the last couple of days, really.

Sarroch goes over to a sideboard and pours me a glass from the pitcher there. He hands it to me. "Can you also find a motorbike that will be suitable for you? Something good for rough terrain and rocks."

"When you mean find something…"

"I mean, find an actual dealer with the bike you want."

"In the Mundane world?"

"Yes, and then show it to me. I'll make it transition into our realm."

"You can do that?"

"Of course."

"Handy. Well, the best kind of bike for that kind of terrain will be a KTM." I whip out my phone, pleasantly surprised to see it has connection. "You guys have Wi-Fi here?"

Sarroch takes a seat in a large and comfortable bamboo chair. "Of course. This is the twenty-first century, even in the werecat realm."

I take another chair, reclining against the cushions and looking up motorbikes. It's been a while since I rode a dirt bike. Not since I left England, in fact. I used to ride them as a teenager, after I met Pree, or Priscilla. She became my best friend after I invited her over to my house for the first time and she suggested we try to dye each other's hair in my parents's bathtub while they were out.

It went horridly wrong, which we found hilarious, and we had such a great time that we were joined at the hip from that day on. Her father ran—well, still runs, as far as I know —a dirt bike race track. She taught me to ride bikes, and we used to ride on her father's track after hours.

I feel a faint pang as I flick through Panong bike dealerships, looking for the kind of bike I need. I never told Pree about the Mayak or the truth of my life in Panong, and as a result we've lost touch a bit these last couple of years, which is a crying shame.

"Ah, here we are." I show Sarroch the website link with the bike that should be suitable for whatever kind of terrain I need to ride on.

"Excellent."

———

SARROCH LEAVES ME TO SORT OUT THE MOTORBIKE AND TO rest. I take a nap, and when I wake up to find someone has left a tray of snacks in the living room, I realise I'm also starving.

I then make use of my deodorant, brush my teeth, and I even floss. All items that are conspicuously missing from the bathroom. Ha—and there he was claiming I'd have everything I'd need, arguing against me bringing a backpack.

I'll have to give Sarroch a lesson in the more prosaic aspects of life as a human. Feeling more than a little smug— who doesn't love being right?—I make a point of leaving my wash bag out on the little shelf above the sink.

By the time I need to leave and go to the race, I'm feeling rested and more than a little excited at the thought of riding a dirt bike again.

Unfortunately, getting to the race involves another death-defying, stomach-curdling jump into the mists that shroud the base of the trees. I make it with only minor squealing—clearly I'm getting used to this new way of travelling.

And it's not actually that bad. We land as if we've just

jumped from a low wall, not from how many hundreds of feet high...

The ground is spongy and littered with leaves, and we're deep in a dark, lush forest that's currently crawling with werecats. For all of Pragya's protests that they're civilised, I was still expecting something primal, having so many hunters gathered together. At the very least, much grunting and roaring as men and women shift from human to feline, a gruesome process in itself, with bones breaking and skin tearing. I thought the air would be thick with the buzzing of magic and with tension as the various large cats sized each other up or maybe even started to fight.

Instead, it's so civilised, it's bordering on sedate.

Those in human forms are disappearing behind modesty screens to shift out of sight. Those already in animal form are nuzzling others in greetings, or in some cases even going as far as to groom one another, eliciting rumbles, chuffs, and purrs of pleasure—depending on the type of large cat.

Only a few stand aside from the socialising, as distant and aloof as cats can be.

The otherworldly twilight continues down here, but the air is cooler and far more humid, smelling of damp earth, mushrooms, and old, decomposing things. There's enough light from the plethora of flowers on the shrubs that grow at ground level to see by, and the ground is littered with dead leaves that rustle beneath my clompy boots—I'm back in my usual threads for the hunt, with a black cropped top and ripped jeans.

The plants around me are unlike anything I've ever seen. Scattered between the behemoths of the tree trunks are enormous ferns that tower taller than me, their delicate fronds tipped with beads of condensed mist that shimmer in the light of the flowers. In fact, most of the plants look old enough to have been brushing against the sides of dinosaurs as they trundled through the forest.

"Your dirt bike should be over here," Sarroch says, gesturing for me to follow.

I follow him over to where, sure enough, a brand new KTM 350 SX-F awaits. It has bright orange bodywork with black accents. Like a tiger version of a dirt bike.

I squeal with excitement, rushing over to it. "Oh my *god,* I didn't actually think you would do it. This is amazing! Wait." I look back at him. "Was this stolen? I've had my fill of trouble, enough to last me a lifetime. So if this was nicked…"

"Of course not. I've had my assistant pay for it."

"Okay, good. If you're able to bring it back to Panong when we're done here, I'll pay you back for it and keep it." My eyes roam over its sleek curves. That is one *hell* of a bike.

"Apiya, I can buy you a bike."

"Hmm?" I tear my eyes away from the sexy piece of machinery before me. "You can, evidently, but whether you may or not is another matter."

"What do you mean?"

"That I don't want you buying me a bike. I'll pay for this. It'll take me a little while, but I'll pay you back."

Sarroch rolls his eyes. "Apiya, money is a human concept. I couldn't care less about it, and if you're going to be part of the Mayak, you have to learn not to care about it as well. All this—the motorbike, the money—they're just part of the daydreams shared by the Mundane collective. We use it when it's useful, but it's not important. It doesn't matter."

"Excellent. I agree, money isn't important. So you won't care that I'm paying you back, because it doesn't matter."

Sarroch opens his mouth to reply, but I raise a hand to stop him. "You don't know me that well, yet, but you'll learn to identify this particular expression." I point at my face. I can't see myself, but I've heard my father refer to my 'more stubborn than a mule' expression numerous times. "This expression is a hint that you should cut your losses, take your own advice about money not mattering, and leave me to do what I want to do with mine."

Sarroch gives me a grudging smile. "Fair enough."

And because he bought me a KTM 350SX-F, I reach up to my tiptoes and kiss him on the cheek. His hand hovers at my hip for a second, his thumb brushing against the skin at my waist, sending a shiver over my nerves.

"Thanks for the bike." My voice has gone husky, the smugness evaporated.

Sarroch holds my eye for a moment and then steps back, removing his hand from my waist. I can still feel a faint tingle from where he touched me.

"I should go change."

I laugh. "You make it sound like you're just going to throw some new clothes on."

"A little more painful than that, unfortunately."

"And you're feeling okay? No hint of the disaster Pragya is expecting?"

"None whatsoever."

"Good."

"Once everyone is ready, they'll give the signal, and you'll see what we're chasing after. You can't miss it. It'll be very bright." He looks the bike over. "And you're sure you know how to ride one of these? You'll be safe?"

"Do I ever? I used to ride dirt bikes as a teenager on this awesome track, doing jumps and tricks." I broke my collar-bone doing one of those tricks, but I'll keep that little fact to myself.

I watch him head over to the screens to change. I really

hope the hunt goes well. It doesn't seem right or fair for Pragya to be holding his past over his head like that, if it's true that there won't ever be a repeat of what happened long ago.

Another small part of me feels a shiver of nerves. Pragya felt like a power in her own right, and she seemed pretty sure something would go wrong. I can't ignore that, either.

Still mulling this over, I grab the jacket that's been laid out for me on the bike's seat. To no one's surprise, it fits me perfectly. I smile. Sarroch may have many faults, but the man knows a thing or two about being smooth.

The helmet matches the bike, and I slip it on, securing it into place. Then I bring the bike off the centre stand and swing my leg over it, turning on the ignition and testing the throttle.

A nearby tiger looks at me, his expression unreadable, before sneezing contemptuously. He's orange and black, with the same huge fangs as Sarroch, the kind that brings to mind a sabre-tooth tiger.

"Yeah, well, I only have two legs, so I need help," I tell the tiger cheerfully. I'm straddling a brand new KTM bike— no amount of feline contempt could sour my mood right now. Plus, now I know that all these supposedly scary weretigers are basically like oversized house cats who like to laze in the sun and do their claws on huge scratching posts.

A smaller cat comes towards me. She has a thick, fluffy tail, and beautiful marbled markings. She sits down when she reaches the front of my bike, looking me and the bike over with her head cocked.

"Pragya?" I guess.

Her ears twitch. Okay, not Pragya.

The little cat comes closer to sniff at the bike and rubs her cheeks against it, marking it with her scent. Then she tosses her head prettily and wanders away, tail high in the air.

Cats.

Finally, Sarroch reappears from behind his screen. Although his tiger is hostile to me, he really is a magnificent creature. His fur is the purest white, striped with black marks. His eyes are the blue of a deep glacier, and his sabre-tooth fangs are huge, gleaming white, and sharp as any dagger.

He's so big, his head reaches the top of my chest, nearly level with my throat. As far as I can see, there's only one other tiger that's bigger than him, a regular orange and black one in the distance.

"Are you ready for the hunt?" I ask Sarroch, pretending I can't sense his tiger's coldness. But it's there, oh so palpable.

Sarroch's tiger looks at me, his gaze short and flat. I frown at him. What the hell is so bad about me that he feels the need to look at me like that? My gut tells me this goes beyond not liking me as a person. It's like I've *done* something to him, although what it is, I have no idea.

A loud roar echoes through the forest, rattling my ribcage, and then a globe of light so bright it's almost painful to look at shoots up in the air.

All the felines follow it with their gaze, their heads snapping up, a collective roar rising up in response. Then they all dart off with astounding, preternatural speed.

I rev the bike and shoot forward after them, disappearing into the gloomy depths of the ancient forest.

9

I t may have been a few years since I've ridden a dirt
bike off-road, but it all comes rushing back. What is it
they say about riding a bike? Sure, they didn't mean a
KTM dirt bike, but the saying clearly holds true in this
instance.

In no time, everything fades away, and I'm left with the
simple exhilaration of the ride.

Pragya hadn't lied before when she said this hunt was
more about a contest of agility than an actual hunt. The ball
of light darts this way and that, often turning back on itself.

The cats are sprinting through the forest, jumping up
into trees for those who can climb well when the ball of
light shoots upwards, or lightly leaping over fallen trunks
and darting between branches. The speed and precision of
their reactions is mind-boggling, to say nothing of their
ability to abruptly change direction without slowing down.

The concentration and skill required of me to keep my
bike more or less level with them has sweat pouring down
my back, but I'm loving every moment of it. All manner of
ferns and other plants I don't recognise, with giant, lush

green leaves, whip my chest and the bike as we plough through them, my tires sending up sprays of dirt and dead leaves when I have to spin around to change direction.

Getting the bike over fallen tree trunks either requires me to peel off to find a rise from which to jump, or I have to detour all the way around the tree. The jumps are by far the more fun option.

A snow leopard leaps from a rock and narrowly misses the ball of light, which darts back, coming straight towards me.

I whoop with excitement, spin my bike around, and open the throttle for all it's worth, racing through the undergrowth after it. For a short, exhilarating moment, I'm at the front of the pack.

A very short moment. The cats catch me up at the first obstacle, zipping past me as I'm forced to slow to swerve. I push the bike up a pile of rocks and leap off the top boulder, landing a pretty tricky jump, and yelling my excitement.

A panther darts across me and I swerve in a great spray of soil and dead leaves to avoid her, braking hard to avoid slamming into a nearby tree.

"Shit."

I look back over my shoulder, panting, my heart hammering. Sarroch's tiger is there, and he looks perfectly calm.

"Look at that!" I call at him. "Pragya got it all wrong. Someone cut me off and you didn't even react. This is going to go perfectly without a hitch."

The tiger twitches his ears and his tail, obviously amused. I grin at him. "Well, come on then."

I swing my bike around and chase after the panther. Sarroch's tiger falls into step with me as the trail has grown wide enough for us to be side by side.

I whoop again, glancing over at him. He's looking at me too, and while it's not exactly friendly, it doesn't seem to imply he'd like to squash me like a cockroach. Progress?

Scratch the question—definite progress. I can sense Sarroch's tiger's enjoyment.

I grin wider. This is so damn cool. Riding through primordial forest with Sarroch's tiger like that, like something out of a film—

The tiger abruptly cuts me off.

I try to swerve, but it's too tight, and the ground is too uneven. The tires spin out from underneath me, and I go flying. I roll a couple of times, and I hear a loud crash.

Panting hard, I slowly push up to kneeling. My sexy new bike is now a smashed up mess wrapped around a small tree. The stinging along my right shin and knee tells me I've left a decent amount of skin on the forest floor.

Thank heavens for my helmet.

Sarroch's tiger is still standing right where he cut me off. I stand up, fuming as I yank my helmet off.

"Sarroch, what the hell are you playing at? That was some stupidly dangerous shit you just pulled! If I hadn't..."

The words die on my lips as I catch sight of his eyes. They're not flat or contemptuous like they were earlier. They're not amused.

Instead, they're completely dead, as if neither Sarroch nor his tiger are there at all.

"Sarroch?"

The tiger lowers his head a little. Around us the forest is utterly silent save for roaring in the distance from the other werecats chasing the light. Sarroch and I are alone.

"Sarroch, quit scaring me," I snap, going for confident, hoping I can shake him out of whatever this is.

Pragya's warning that something would go wrong rings in my ears.

A low growl rises up in the tiger's throat. Soft and so low it feels like it's rising from the underworld. Everything in my body screams at me to get out of here. It's not just finding myself alone with a predator. My intuition is blaring at me that something is wrong. Very, very, deeply and totally wrong.

"Sarroch? What's going on?" My voice sounds frightened, uncertain. I take a step back. The silence is thick, like the mist has swallowed the rest of the world, and there's a pressure in the air that pushes against my ears.

The growling rumbles lower, the tiger slowly coming to a crouching position. The kind of a position a tiger stalking a prey takes before pouncing.

His eyes are still totally and terrifyingly blank. What had Sarroch said earlier? That he isn't a monster? And yet that's how he looks right now. Like a monster.

Pragya was right.

A drop of cold sweat traces a line along my spine, and a sick fear crawls through my stomach. Never taking my eyes off him, I peel off my left glove, the silver under the skin of my left hand the only defence I have. I left all of my razors in my backpack.

Stupid, stupid, stupid.

My fingers are shaking. I'm no match for Sarroch. My best hope is to hold out until someone can get here to help me.

Still, he stays as he is, watching me with his cold, dead eyes.

I'm trying to decide whether I have a better shot if I run or stay still when he pounces. It's so fast, I don't even see it happening.

One second I'm standing, the next I'm screaming in fear, hot pain lacerating my right shoulder, my left hand, the one with the silver under the skin, thrusting forward.

The stench of burning hair rises up and the tiger roars in pain. And then he's off me.

I scramble to my feet, panting hard. Another tiger, this one orange and black and smaller, shoots out of the forest and comes to stop between us. She looks from Sarroch and to me questioningly until her eyes land on the wound at my shoulder. Her eyes narrow.

I look back at Sarroch's tiger, but now his eyes look normal again. He's also breathing heavily, and his own eyes are wide, confused. The newly arrived tiger shakes her head once, her tail twitching angrily.

Then with a grunt, she begins to shift.

10

I t takes a few minutes for both her and Sarroch to change, minutes during which I don't turn away. I'm not allowing anyone to be at my back right now.

The change is definitely a lot quicker here than what I remember from Sarroch shifting back in the Mundane world, but I suppose that makes sense. They're in their own realm now, steeped in their own magic.

"What happened?" Pragya asks curtly the moment her change is complete.

Both she and Sarroch are now in human form and naked. Neither of them seems at all fazed by that fact, and I'm careful to keep my gaze at eye level.

Sarroch is pale. "I...I don't know. Apiya, are you okay? Your shoulder... What happened? What..."

I frown at him. "You don't remember?"

He goes nearly green at the implication of my question.

Seeing him look so normal, and having Pragya standing nearby, close enough that I can feel her power, goes a long way towards making me feel safe.

"What do you remember?" I ask Sarroch. "We were

running side by side—well, running and riding side by side."

"Yes. I remember that. My tiger was surprisingly enjoying the moment."

"And then?"

His gaze dips down to his chest where my silver would have touched him, although the burn has already healed. "Then you're burning my tiger and he's throwing himself back off you." He looks scared. "What did I do?"

"You—well, your tiger—cut me off. That's why I crashed." I gesture at the bike that is now wrapped around a tree. "And then you...Your eyes were wrong. Very wrong. Like they were dead, and you weren't there anymore. Not you, not your tiger."

Pragya lets out a hiss of shock.

"Possession," she mutters.

I whirl to face her. "You expected this to happen? Is that why you insisted we do this hunt? Dangling me as some kind of bait?" My voice is clipped and harsh with anger.

She shakes her head. "I thought Sarroch would try to attack another werecat if someone got too close or put you in danger. I thought he had unprocessed memories that he held on to."

"You mean like PTSD?"

"Sort of. A magical equivalent. I never expected that he might attack you, or I wouldn't have left you in such a vulnerable position."

Sarroch crouches slowly down, running both hands over his face and hair. "I attacked you." His voice is strained. He looks devastated.

"Well, it sounds like it wasn't you, but something that took over," I reply cautiously. "And I'm fine."

He points at my skinned leg and at my bleeding shoulder.

"Superficial," I reply. "Give it a couple of weeks and it will all be sorted." I look at Pragya. "You said that what happened was a possession. What does that mean?"

"It means that you both need to come to my hut right away."

Sarroch nods and stands again. "Absolutely."

"And you will allow me to examine you?" Pragya asks him.

"Yes. Of course." He throws me a pleading look. "If I had any idea that something like this might happen, I never would have refused. This has never happened before. Never. Not since..." He rubs two hands over his face. "I can't believe I attacked you. I'm so sorry, Apiya. I'm so sorry. Magic help me."

Seeing the devastation on his features does more to reassure me than Pragya's explanation that he's been possessed by something.

"Sarroch, I'm fine. I'm okay. Let's get to Pragya's hut and see what's going on."

————

ONCE SARROCH AND PRAGYA ARE CLOTHED, WE MAKE OUR WAY back up into the trees—the jumping magic, if that's what it's called, works to go up as well as down—and Pragya leads the way to a platform that's set apart from the rest of the suspended tree city, and so low down, it's half-swallowed by the mist.

It's definitely cooler here—not quite as cool and humid as down at ground level, but the air doesn't have the same liquid warmth quality to it as it does in the upper levels. I can actually feel the mist against my skin as I move, the humidity parting like a thousand invisible spiderwebs against my face.

Pragya's hut is made from vertical bamboo poles with a thatched roof of dry palm fronds. The bamboo poles aren't pressed together in order to form solid walls. Instead, there are small gaps between them in a way that almost brings to mind a cage.

I say almost because the space between the bamboo is occupied by small carved objects that are strung on thread so fine it's almost invisible. Some look to be bone, some wood, some metal. They click and tap gently against each other and against the bamboo as the breeze rocks them from side to side.

Every object makes a slightly different sound so that it's kind of like the house is playing music. It's pretty in a slightly otherworldly way, but it wouldn't take much for it to shift from pretty to creepy.

"Come in," Pragya says, opening the door.

Before I can reply, I feel a warm, crawling sensation along the back of my neck, and glance back. Sarroch has frozen near the rope bridge that we crossed to reach the platform. There's a terrible confusion on his face, mixed with fear and struggle.

Emotions flash on his face, including for one frightening moment pure loathing as he looks at me. That look is almost immediately removed to make way for more shame, fear, and more confusion.

"Come in." Pragya's voice is more powerful this time, and I find myself walking towards the hut before I've even realised I decided to do so. I look at her—her eyes are large and dark.

When I next blink, we're all inside her hut. At least that's where I'm assuming we are—I don't actually remember crossing the threshold.

As with so many Mayak spaces, the inside of the hut is far larger than the outside should allow. Maybe it's something like a Mayak space within Mayak space, like some immense nesting dolls. Which makes sense, given how back in the baku realm, there were memories within memories within memories.

Although there are gaps between every bamboo pole making up the walls, the air feels stale and stuffy as if it can't circulate in from the outside. It's also uncomfortably warm. No light penetrates from the outside in spite of the gaps within the walls. Instead, dishes of oil are scattered throughout, their surface burning, but the flames don't emit any smoke. They cast a flickering yellow light on everything.

I should have noticed the yellow glow of flames from outside because it should have seeped through the gaps between the bamboo poles. No great surprise that magic is involved.

The actual furnishings of the room, or the hut, are a real holder's paradise. Ilmu would approve. All manner of things are scattered about in untidy piles, on the floor, or just haphazardly strewn about the furniture. Skulls—human, animal, and quite possibly magical. Feathers, bones, and bowls of something that looks like teeth and claws. I don't want to look too much closer.

Oddly enough, while there are parchments covered in arcane symbols scattered about the room, there isn't a single pen, quill, or any source of ink that I can see.

More importantly, now that we're here, Pragya looks and feels vastly more powerful than she had back outside. We're on her territory here, that much is clear.

"Sit," she tells Sarroch, who is still hovering by the door.

He doesn't look happy at all to be here. His eyes aren't quite dead like they were before, but they're flat and cold.

"Hold on," he says suddenly. "We're basing all this on what Apiya says, but how do we know that's even right? What if she simply crashed her bike?"

I'm surprised at how much that hurts. "And the claw marks at my shoulder?" I ask him acidly.

Sarroch winces, and his eyes clear, looking concerned. He takes a step forward, and then the same coldness as before descends once again.

Pragya is right. Something is taking some kind of control of him.

"I can sort this out myself," Sarroch announces. "I don't need your help, old woman."

He spins on his heels and goes to march out of the hut.

All of a sudden, the pressure in the air increases tenfold, making my ears pop. When Pragya speaks, her voice is both soft and yet at the same time, so strong and powerful it rings deep within my bones. And it's rich with so much magic, I can feel it buzzing against my skin.

"You will not leave this place until you have either let me examine you or you have killed Apiya," she thunders.

Kill Apiya? Say what, now?

11

T he power that fills the small hut feels every bit as dangerous as the pressure of a gathering storm. My hair is rising up, pulled by the static that now crowds the air, which smells of ozone. Sarroch has frozen, his back still to the both of us.

I don't dare look into Pragya's eyes, but from my peripheral vision it's clear that they've gone huge and black like the way Sarroch's had gone when he'd tried to hypnotise me in the past.

"If you leave now," Pragya continues in that impossibly soft and yet thundering voice, "You will never be able to form a mating bond with Apiya, and the Mayak Elders will execute her. If she is to die, then you will kill her *yourself*, rather than shame us all by allowing her to die through cowardice." The last word cracks in the air, seeming to hang around long after Pragya has spoken it.

Sarroch turns around slowly. I barely recognise him. His facial muscles are twitching, his hands and shoulders are shaking. Emotions seem to be flickering onto his face and disappearing just as fast, and he seems to be going through a massive internal fight.

I take a cautious step back, the skin crawling up my spine in warning.

He makes a strained grunt, and all of a sudden something clears. The pressure disappears from the air, as if it deflated like a balloon, and Sarroch's face settles back to something normal, something I can recognise.

He takes a deep, shuddering breath and walks back to Pragya. "You know what it is? What is taking a hold of me?" He looks over at me. "That wasn't me, just now. Something... Something is controlling my emotions."

Pragya regards him carefully. "I think I have an inkling."

"You can do something about it?"

"I can try. Sit. Both of you." She turns away and starts rooting around in a canvas sack.

Sarroch sits cross-legged on one of the floor cushions. I take another one, but I stay on my guard.

"I'm sorry, Apiya," he whispers.

"I know," I reply in much the same tone. "You're more powerful than he is?" I ask Pragya more loudly. This is the kind of information I need right now, because it would be pretty helpful to have someone around who can control Sarroch if the possession happens again.

"My Compelling is," Pragya replies, still searching.

She seems relaxed, but I don't miss the implication— that while her compelling is stronger than Sarroch's, the rest of her magic might very well not be.

Pragya has obviously found what she wanted, because she turns back to face us. In her right hand, she's holding what looks like...

"Is that a shoulder blade?" I ask.

"Yes. The scapula of an ox." She looks over at Sarroch. "I

should have known when you never took another mate since Eyva passed."

Sarroch frowns. "I made a vow..."

"No one keeps that kind of vow for so long," Pragya interrupts. "Thousands of years, and you never loved another?"

Sarroch shifts uncomfortably and shrugs. "I suppose I never found someone to replace her."

Pragya raises an eyebrow. "I'm sure some people would find that romantic. But I think the thing that took over and made you attack Apiya is the same thing that's stopping you from taking another mate."

"Stopping me how?"

"Let me have a look at you and I'll tell you."

Sarroch squirms with discomfort as she squats down in front of him, holding the shoulder blade in her right hand and a viciously sharp spike in her right. Leather coils around the end of it forming a handle of sorts, allowing her to grip it securely.

Pragya begins to mutter as her eyes roam over him. Then they flutter shut, but not quite all the way, so the whites are still showing. Her left hand begins to scratch symbols into the shoulder blade with the spike, moving jerkily as if somebody else has grabbed hold of her hand and is moving it for her.

She stops abruptly, reopens her eyes, and stands up. She fetches a small cast-iron dish, places the scapula inside it, and hands it to Sarroch. "If you'd be so kind. Just one moment, before we begin." From one of her messy shelves, she pulls out a sturdy looking grey feather.

"It would be best if you stood," she tells Sarroch, who obeys. "Good. Now let us begin."

Sarroch cradles the cast iron dish in both hands, and it

starts to glow orange. Even from where I'm standing, I can feel the heat rolling off the iron, but Sarroch doesn't seem to feel any pain as he holds it.

The dish heats up further until it starts to glow white. I have to look away—the metal is burning so bright, it's painful to behold. And then there's an almighty crack.

The shoulder blade has broken in half and from between the two parts, a thick, greasy smoke rises up.

Pragya hums and mutters words as she wafts at the smoke towards Sarroch with her feather, moving to his front and to his back, helping the smoke spread all around him. It slowly turns into a nebulous cocoon.

When the smoke starts to clear, Pragya heads over to the wall where a large rectangle of blood-red fabric is hanging. She yanks the fabric away, revealing a huge mirror behind it.

Sarroch makes a shocked, raspy noise, dropping the dish to the floor. It turns black and cold even before it hits the floorboards and clangs dully, spilling out the broken pieces of shoulder blade. Sarroch doesn't notice any of it. His eyes are wide, his mouth hangs open as he stares at the mirror.

"No..." He breathes, taking half a step towards the mirror and then stopping.

In the hut, Sarroch still looks unchanged. But in the mirror, some kind of grey and bloated parasite clings to him, its mouth buried in his neck so much so that it's not visible. It has a huge, distended belly, and the tiniest throat, so small it would rival a wasp's waist. Its arms and legs can barely be called that, little more than translucent grey ribbons that are wrapped around him. It has huge dark eyes that are all black, without any white to give them a human appearance.

"A hungry ghost," I whisper in shock.

Hungry ghosts are condemned to spend eternity with

huge bellies and tiny mouths and throats, so they can never swallow enough to fill the voids they carry inside them.

I realise, then, that this one has long hair. Thin strands that float around its head. In fact, the whole ghost floats gently as if it were suspended in water, or wafted about by a small breeze. There are a few other signs—like a hint of what could be construed as breasts—to make me think this ghost is female.

"It's not possible." Sarroch has gone grey. "I did all the rites when I buried her. I went through all the rituals to let go of her."

"But when did you do the rituals and the rites?" Pragya asks. "Before, or after your rampage?"

He looks sick. "After." His voice is barely audible.

Pragya sighs. "If I'd had any inkling of how bad things were, I'd never have let you avoid me for so long. I thought you were chained by your memories, which is fixable, but this...This is bad."

"Can you free her?" Sarroch asks, his voice raw.

"I'm not sure. I have never heard of a hungry ghost being allowed to remain for such a long period of time. Nor of one that has become so powerful it is able to not only cling to its host, but influence the host's behaviour, as well. It will be feeding on your joy, your ability to love, to care for another. Given that you have never loved another since Eyva, it will likely be feeding on any positive emotions you harbour towards others. It might also be feeding *you* emotions, which explains any abrupt mood changes like what happened in the forest."

"She," Sarroch says tightly, clenching his fists, but still not removing his eyes from the mirror. "*She*."

"No. It. Eyva is gone. What remains is not Eyva. This is not Eyva's spirit, not her soul, it is nothing of her. All that is left is an aberration, a perversion caused by events that should never have happened. This is nothing more than a greedy, bottomless pit given shape, and it is as much of a parasite as a tick is on a regular tiger."

Sarroch closes his eyes briefly, although they snap open almost immediately, as if he can't bear to take them away from the ghost hanging to him for too long. "So this is the price I paid for my actions," he whispers.

"I didn't think the Mayak dead came back as ghosts?" I ask.

"They don't. Not normally. It can happen, but it's very, very rare. I wasn't alive back then, so I cannot say for sure what happened. My guess would be that during those days when Sarroch lost control and went on the rampage, he clung on too tightly to Eyva, rather than letting her go, and maybe she to him. That would have been bad enough, but to do so in a time of such... violence, such vast amounts of magic being unleashed on the world... I'm not sure what exactly would have caused a hungry ghost to be created, but the lack of proper rituals for all those days would definitely have been a part of it. Some part of Eyva didn't pass through the veil, but instead it stayed and became this perversion. It's also very possible there was no one around at the time who was able to address that problem. Or who was willing to."

And I'm guessing other than Mr Sangong who apparently was somehow able to stop Sarroch, no one would have wanted to get close to him after he had wiped out an entire civilisation in a few days.

"Why is the hungry ghost taking over now?" I ask. "Sarroch hasn't attacked me before."

"It will be more powerful here, in our realm. Our magic is in everything, in the very air. That will feed it." Pragya looks at Sarroch. "Was your tiger enjoying himself, just before he attacked Apiya?"

Sarroch gives a single, miserable nod, still unable to remove his eyes from the parasite attached to him.

"That will have been why. Sarroch's tiger's emotions will be stronger, more immediate. If he enjoyed himself with Apiya, the hungry ghost may have picked up on it. Here, in our realm, it might be powerful enough to have basic emotions itself, like jealousy."

Sarroch gives a pained grunt, his body spasming. Then his body spasms again.

"Apiya, stand back," Pragya snaps at me, thrusting a hand out towards me in warning.

"What's going on?" I ask with alarm as I retreat until my back is pressed against the wall.

Sarroch collapses to the floor, groaning in pain, his spine rounding until it looks like it might snap. And then it does.

"His tiger is forcing the shift on him," Pragya replies.

"Can he do that?"

"Sometimes. It's rare for our tigers to take over, but when it happens, it's best not to interfere. Whilst Sarroch is a rational man, his tiger is likely to be *extremely* affected by all this." She waves at the mirror. "Don't go near him."

Sarroch's body begins to break, the skin and clothing along his spine splitting. The rest of his clothing tears from the force of it, making him roar, maybe from the pain of it.

Pragya is also standing well back, but she doesn't look afraid, which reassures me greatly.

It only takes a couple of minutes before Sarroch's tiger is lying on the ground, panting heavily. He lifts his head up towards the mirror.

The hungry ghost is still there, fluttering softly in her

invisible breeze. Her arms and legs are wrapped around the tiger, her mouth buried in his fur.

Sarroch's tiger makes a soft, pained sound in his throat, crawling towards the mirror on his belly. His icy blue eyes are wide, staring at the ugly grey parasite that floats alongside his own reflection. Again he makes a soft keening sound.

"I'm sorry, Sarroch," Pragya says softly, walking over to a nearby table. "I'm sorry I didn't push you to do this before. That I didn't see what was wrong until now. Arrogance will have clouded my judgement—I thought I knew what was happening. I was wrong." She has reached the table, and she grabs something, turning back to face the tiger. "Cutting her out will hurt, there's no way around it. But it must be done."

In her left hand is a beautiful dagger. The handle is delicately carved gold with emeralds shaped like tears in the pommel and guard. The blade is silver, with a ridge running down the middle. Two long tears run alongside the ridge, merging with it.

Sarroch's tiger snaps his head to her, his growl low and menacing.

"Sarroch." Pragya's voice cracks like a whip. "It must be done, and you know it. You cannot allow that thing to remain. It is far too dangerous to continue giving it the power to influence your behaviour. To say nothing of the fact that it is an aberration. A perversion. It *must* be removed."

And then in the mirror I see the hungry ghost push its head into the tiger's, so that all that is visible is the distended belly and ribbon like arms and legs.

The tiger's eyes seem to slip aside, replaced with that

completely empty, dead look I've seen before. He turns to look at Pragya.

Pragya's own eyes go wide with fear, and her nostrils flare. "Run!" she shouts.

But before I can move, the world explodes into a million tiny fragments.

12

My reflexes kick in, and I curl into the tightest ball I can, arms up over my head, chin down to protect my face. My knees are curled up in front of my chest to protect my soft abdomen.

Tiny, razor-sharp fragments are flying everywhere, slicing me open with a thousand tiny cuts. My jeans and jacket only hold out for a short moment before I start to feel the cuts on my skin. The pressure building up all around makes it hard to breathe, the feeling as if someone was trying to tear the very air in half.

"Sarroch! *Sarroch!!*" I scream, my eyes squeezed shut, trying to snap him out of it. I'm terrified that something might get past my arms and blind me.

And then the awful pressure in the air slides into my body. It's like I've been reduced to nothing more than cells and atoms, and some unstoppable force is seeping into and between them, trying to pry them apart.

No, no, no!

I don't scream that, though, I just think it, because my voice isn't working. My magic scrambles madly, desperately trying to keep all of me together in one piece. But I can feel the pressure building, and building, and I know that if I let go for one moment, every part of me will explode outwards the same way the hut was just pulverised.

I hold on tight, as tight as I can, but there's too much of me, too many parts of me, and I lack the strength and the skill. I can feel my control giving way ever so slowly, like a single-handed grip on a greasy steel bar, slowly, gradually, slipping.

Everything inside me is screaming in panic. I can't reach out with my magic to try to get to Sarroch. I can do nothing to influence or stop the position I'm in. To do any of that would mean letting go of myself and allowing myself to be destroyed.

No matter how much I strain and try, I can't stop the gradual invasion of that terrible, terrible pressure slowly prying me apart.

My final grip on control breaks, and for an awful, terrifying moment I feel myself suspended, in what I know is the fraction of the second before everything explodes outwards, before my existence finishes. I'm no longer a body, just a collection of tiny particles in space that are gathered just before they are scattered on the wind. I have no sensation left. My consciousness feels like a tiny blip, a fragile candle flame about to be snuffed out.

A huge, warm breath suddenly floods me, and as it does it gathers all of me, down to every last to cell and molecule, bringing me back to myself, so that I'm suddenly once again a solid body curled on the floor.

I recognise that breath. It was the same huge breath I felt flood me when I was fighting for my life after Yue ripped part of my neck open, back in my kitchen. It was the same breath that pushed the sea into an almighty wave back when Ari and I were Nerong's prisoners.

Qinglong.

I feel a brief sense of a vastness beyond the scope of my comprehension, and then she's gone.

It takes me a couple more moments before I realise that the dangerous whirl of razor-sharp things that were cutting me has also stopped.

I gingerly lift my head just enough to get a glimpse of what's going on around me.

There's nothing left. I'm surrounded by total and utter destruction. It's not just that things have been smashed or broken, the way they would have been if a human had come along to try to break the hut. It's like everything just... Disintegrated into the tiniest fragment. Into powder in some places. The only thing that remains unscathed, without so much as a scratch on it, is the blade of the silver dagger Pragya wanted to use to cut the hungry ghost away from Sarroch. It rests atop a small pile of pulverised debris.

Despite what Sarroch and others have said, I still hadn't realised the sheer scale of the destructive power he can wield.

I raise my head fully. The panic when my eyes meet the tiger's icy blue ones freezes the squeal of fear in my throat.

I have just about enough awareness to notice that his eyes are normal, not blank and dead. They look at me, wide and anguished. He shakes his head, stepping back over the remains of the hut, as if trying to clear his vision of what he's seeing.

"Go..."

The voice that croaks the word doesn't sound human. Both of us look over at Pragya. She's still in one piece, but just looking at her is painful. It's not the blood – she's bleeding from her ears, nose, eyes, and mouth, and like me, she has a lot of tiny cuts, but no big wounds.

Rather, her body looks like it has been so broken, it barely has a human-shaped anymore. Her arms and legs are bent in impossible ways, as is her spine, and there's something seriously wrong with her ribcage, which looks half caved in.

"Go..."

Sarroch's tiger lets out a roar filled with anguish.

"Go now."

Sarroch's tiger lowers his head. He throws me a single pleading look, and then he leaps off the platform and down into the mist.

———

I STAND UP, WANTING TO RUSH TO PRAGYA'S SIDE, BUT MY BODY chooses that moment to remind me what it has been subjected to. It's not the cuts, the wound at my shoulder, my skinned leg. My whole body feels like I've been hit by a double-decker bus that was loaded with cannonballs.

Instead of standing up and hurrying to Pragya's side, I stumble back down to my knees and end up crawling awkwardly over.

"What can I do?" I ask her. Stupid to ask her when she can barely speak. "I will go get help."

"Stay... Secret... I...shift."

"Stay... You don't want me to get help? You want to keep this a secret?"

Pragya blinks once.

"Okay, then what can I—" I nearly gag as the shift takes over her body, her already mutilated bones breaking all over again. Unlike her transformation earlier, this isn't swift. It's agonisingly slow, Pragya's struggle obvious. I stand watch over her, frustratingly helpless.

Half an hour. Half an hour of joints popping, bones breaking, muscles tearing and reshaping, before her tigress lies before me, her flank heaving as she pants heavily.

I know enough of weretigers to know they heal better in tiger form, so she must have shifted to deal with her injuries, although I can still see that many remain present. Some of her bones don't look right.

I quash down the urge to go and get someone, but that doesn't change the fact that she needs help. She has a lot of healing to do, and to do that will require energy. Energy means food.

"Pragya, you need food and water. I'll go in search of some. Will you be okay if I leave?"

She raises her head a fraction to look at me and sneezes. Then she turns it ever so slightly to look to her left.

Beyond the destruction, the pulverised remains of her hut, a wide branch is now visible, extending towards a small platform, half hidden in the gloom and the mist. All of it was out of sight before, behind the hut.

"Okay, food and water are there. Got it." I stand on wobbly legs, taking deep breaths. The branch is wide, but not *that* wide. And more importantly, there are no handrails, no safety fences to stop someone from slipping over the edge and falling.

I wouldn't like to walk across the branch at the best of time, even less so now, when I feel about as weak as a drowned kitten, and as in control of my movements as Bambi on ice.

I walk over to the start of the branch where it meets the platform edge. I get on all fours and start crawling across. I'm sure there are people out in the world who would be badass enough to take the risk of running across the branch. I don't care about badass, nor do I care about pride. I care about survival. If I fall, that won't help Pragya, and I have no idea whether I can survive falling into the mist if I do it alone. So crawling it is.

I progress across the branch as fast as I can, doing my best to prevent the pain from the myriad of cuts on my hands and knees from slowing me down. The tree branches are obviously not quite as smooth as the trunk, and I can feel every ridge of the bark in my shredded hands and knees, making the tiny cuts sting like hell. My skinned leg feels like it's on fire, and it's throbbing hard.

In ancient China, a chosen method of execution was death by a thousand cuts. After today, I'll be able to tell my dad that I now know what that particular form of torture feels like.

As stupid as it is, that thought cheers me up a little and distracts me, giving me the boost I need to make it to the other side. I reach the platform, relieved when I can finally stand back on my two feet again. There's a tiny hut here, smaller than Pragya's hut had been. There's no door, just a curtain, and I brush it aside, stepping into the gloom.

Inside, it once again has no bearing on the outside space. It's so cold, I gasp, the air momentarily snatched from my lungs. It's like I've just stepped into a giant fridge. The light is low, so low that I can barely see. I have to hold the curtain open to let a little light filter through.

There's a single set of shelves running along the walls, at an oddly low level. Open sacks of something are lined up on the shelves, but for some reason, the sacks are lopsided. They have a single handle that dangles down over the edge of the shelf.

I grab one and peer inside, to be met with the rich smell

of raw meat. A lot of raw meat. And now the shelves and sacks make sense. They're designed for a tiger to be able to grab them easily. This must be Pragya's personal food stash. Since Sarroch mentioned feeding was a private affair among werecats, maybe each werecat here has their own personal stash, so they can eat in privacy.

I grab two bags. Looking around some more, I also find dishes on the floor full of water. I'll have to do another trip to carry one of those back. It's going to be enough of a challenge going back with the meat as it is.

IT TAKES ME A WHILE, BUT EVENTUALLY I HAVE PRAGYA FED and watered. I have to crawl back and forth on the branch to give her more meat, and fetching the water is a trial in the extreme, one where, for a moment, I think I'm going to tip over the edge. Luckily I make it, and it's heartening to see the healing already taking place in Pragya.

I stay with her for the duration, watching over her as the magic in her body heals whatever damage it is that Sarroch has done to her. I bring the water over when she looks at it, or bring her more meat when she needs to eat more.

I'm feeling incredibly grateful that she's enough of a power in her own right to have been able to survive Sarroch's onslaught. I realise that following that logic makes me a power, but of course the only reason I made it is because Qinglong intervened. *She* is a power, not me.

Every so often I look up, as if somehow I'd be able to see her above—but of course there is no sky here, just canopy and glowing flowers. If I reach out cautiously with my magic, though, I can feel that sense of vastness overhead. I can't get anything more than that. Like she's too big and too powerful for my senses to perceive. But still, feeling her up in the sky is weirdly comforting. I wonder if she watches over me the whole time, or her attention gets drawn to me if I'm in distress or something.

When Pragya finally gets up, it's a relief. She still looks weak, moving stiffly, as if in pain. But she is up on her feet at least. She pads towards me and leans against my side. She's so strong that I nearly topple over.

"What do you need?" I ask her. "Are you able to change back to human now?"

She shakes her head and sneezes. Then she leans against me again.

"Stop that, or I'll end up falling."

She shifts and nudges my leg with her head. Then she stands alongside me again and nudges me with her body.

"Okay, you're going to need to give me more of a hint, because right now, the only meaning I can make of this is that you want me to ride you, which I know isn't right." I haven't forgotten Sarroch's obvious disgust at the thought of being ridden.

But Pragya nods her head once, looking at me more insistently, and pushing a little bit harder against my leg.

"You want me to ride you? Seriously?"

Her ears twitch. She's getting annoyed.

"Hold on, I thought weretigers didn't like being ridden. Why exactly do you want me to ride you?"

She looks over at the mist.

"Ah. Because I need to do that in order to successfully make the jump?"

She dips her head and then gives an impatient twitch to her tail.

"We're going to go look for Sarroch, aren't we?" I take a

breath. I want to know that he's okay, and we need to sort out that hungry ghost issue. But I can't help a trill of fear.

I reach up, this time a little more confidently, searching for the presence up in the sky, and hoping that if things go bad again, Qinglong will be able to intervene.

Then I gather my courage with both hands, and trying to be as careful as I can, clamber up onto Pragya's back.

She pads over to the edge of the platform and jumps off.

13

We land softly, as I had before with Sarroch. Pragya doesn't even pause, breaking into a powerful run, so surefooted and fleet, you'd think she was running on smooth tarmac, not through thick forest underbrush, the ground torn up by roots, rocks, and fallen branches.

I hold on as best I can. I don't ride horses, but even if I did, I don't know how much of a help it would be in riding a tiger. I cling to her neck with both arms, squeezing my knees around her ribcage. Still, I'm bouncing around with all the grace of a sack of proverbial.

When Pragya lets out a low growl, I guess that means I'm holding on too tight, so I let go a touch, which just means I bounce harder.

By the time she stops my legs and bum feel like they have been pummelled by rocks. I climb down gingerly, both for the sake of my posterior and because I'm aware that it must have caused Pragya just as much pain, if not more, given her injuries.

We're on the edge of a lake, diagonal shafts of sunlight slipping through gaps in the canopy to play and shimmer on the water's surface. Heavy ferns trail their fronds through the preternaturally blue water. They're of such a dark green that, in contrast with the brilliance of the sunlight shafts, they look almost black. The rest of the forest crowds around the edges of the water, vines and lianas reaching down towards the blue, as if tentatively attempting to take over this space as well.

A number of dead, regular sized trees poke out of the middle of the lake, spreading their black and leafless branches towards the sunlight. The water looks turbid, almost too thick to just be water. As if it might have been the primordial ooze from of which all of life originated. The smell of damp and rotten things that permeates the forest is stronger here, with a rich metallic undertone. It smells of green, growing things. Of things that crawl and wriggle in the mud.

Sarroch is sitting on a rock over to the right. His knees are pulled tight to his chest, the sunlight's reflection on the water playing on his face. It's hard to equate the man before me with the being who came so close to pulling me apart cell by cell.

Something thuds softly against my hip. Pragya nudges me again and then looks at Sarroch.

I nod and head towards him. I hear her grunt behind me as she begins to shift again.

"Probably best for you to stay where you are." He turns to look at me. His eyes are surrounded by deep purple rings that make them look bruised. His skin has a sickly grey tinge to it, his features drawn. "I'm so sorry," he whispers. "You know I never would have... That if I had control I wouldn't have."

"I know. I saw her. It. The hungry ghost. It stuck its head into yours. I saw it take you over. It wasn't your fault, Sarroch."

Sarroch looks away again. "I don't remember any of it. I just remember coming to and seeing..." He runs a shaking hand over his eyes as if it might erase the sight. "It was like waking up after the last time, all those centuries ago. Waking up to find a world destroyed."

"What actually happened?" I ask, cautiously making my way closer to him. The way I figure, if I can get myself within reach, then if his eyes go again, I can touch him with my silver hand. That seemed to work last time. "I thought you had abilities with metal. How did you do what you did?"

"There's metal in everything, Apiya." He sounds tired. "In your body there's iron, zinc, potassium, magnesium...I don't have close to the same level of control with such small traces, but I'm still able to manipulate them. It's very difficult for me to do, but I can, if I really push it, take all those tiny traces of a metal that exist in every living thing, and pull them apart. It's how I wiped out an entire civilisation in such a short space of time." He buries his head in his hands, fingers digging into his hair. "At least I was somehow able to regain control this time." He takes a long, ragged breath and looks over at me. "I'll make arrangements so you can take someone else as a mate and get your protection from the Mayak Elders that way." He looks up at me. "I *will* make this right by you, Apiya. I will see to it that you are safe, and that your life is provided for, whatever you need."

"What about you? What will happen..."

"It's clear I can never leave the weretiger realm, now. I'm too dangerous."

"It's quite the opposite," Pragya says. I start at the sound of her voice—she changed back much quicker than I expected. "You're too dangerous to stay here." She sounds pained, exhausted. She also has bruises around her eyes, and when she tries to stand she doesn't quite make it, falling clumsily back on all fours.

Sarroch looks like she has just hit him.

"We have our young, here. We cannot take the risk that you might destroy some or all of them."

He nods. "Yes, of course. You're right."

"I'm sorry, Sarroch. If I'd had any idea of how bad things were, I never would have let you avoid me for so long. Had the hungry ghost been dealt with earlier, it wouldn't be so powerful."

"Had I known there was something I never would have avoided you for so long," Sarroch replies.

"In your defence, it's very possible the hungry ghost also had an impact on that, since coming to see me would have been detrimental to its survival. However, it looks like coming to see me had another, unexpected consequence. This has never happened before, right?"

"No." Sarroch looks horrified. "Never. I told you, Pragya. I haven't lost control since that day."

"Then it might be that because our realm is thick with our magic, it also made the hungry ghost more powerful, giving it something else to feed off, which is why it is suddenly able to take you over. I am not a ruler of the underworld to understand the magic of the dead, so this is just an educated guess."

"But it makes sense," I say. "There have been a myriad of opportunities for the hungry ghost to provoke an attack on me before today. It also seems to have more influence when Sarroch is in tiger form, which matches with what you told me earlier, Pragya."

Sarroch nods tiredly. "I agree with both of you, and so

does my tiger. Everything you say makes sense, Pragya. I will leave. You can inform everyone that I will go into a self-imposed exile. If I could ask you to ensure that Apiya is seen to so she can become a part of the Mayak, I would be greatly in your debt."

"Of course," Pragya replies.

I frown. "Sarroch, I'm not just going to stay here while you get exiled."

"That is exactly what you must do."

"No bloody way. The whole speech I gave you before about the fact that I don't just stand by when a friend is in trouble isn't just something that I reserve for other people, you know."

"It should be. You don't help out monsters, you run away from them."

I roll my eyes. "Seriously, not the time to throw yourself a pity party. You had the right of it before—you're not a monster, Sarroch. You have a problem, a parasite, but that's not cause to start pulling out the pitchforks quite yet."

"But I might attack you again," he replies, his voice rising with frustration.

"Firstly, I decide what risks and dangers I'm prepared to take. Secondly, so long as I'm in close proximity to you, I think I can stop that, the way I did in the forest." I touch him with a finger, allowing the silver to rise up to my skin.

It makes a hissing sound, and Sarroch winces, jerking away from me.

"See? But more to the point, we need to sort out this hungry ghost, and you'll clearly need help to do that. I'm not just letting you walk away to deal with this on your own."

"But I don't even have the first idea of what to do or where to start in order to take care of this."

"Well, I figure we go straight to the root of the problem.

Pragya mentioned that a guardian of the underworld would know more about this, so why don't we go and see one of them?"

"That doesn't work. If we do that, Berata Kala will know that it's not possible for me to have chosen you as mate."

I grimace. "Ah, yeah." Berata Kala is one of the Mayak Elders, and one very vocally in favour of condemning me to death for killing Chizu. If he finds out that Sarroch cannot take a mate because of a parasitic hungry ghost, then the Elders will know that we lied, which might very well mean execution for me. I'm not completely sure of this, but it's not a chance I'm particularly willing to take.

"That's a shame," Pragya said softly. "Going to the underworld is a good idea." She glances at Sarroch. "I hope you realise how fortunate you are to have someone willing to stick by you in light of the situation. There aren't many who would do that."

"Oh, I am well aware, but I'm still going to do my best to convince her not to do that."

I wave a hand impatiently to dismiss the idea. "You won't get anywhere, Sarroch. So drop it. Okay, so if we can't get to the underworld through one of the guardians in Asia, what about in Europe? The idea of multiple underworlds is a human concept, right? So surely that should mean that we can get into contact with one of the European guardians, get to the underworld that way, and..." I turned to Pragya. "Do what exactly?"

"I'm not sure. But whatever tiny scrap of Eyva still remains to keep this hungry ghost alive, it needs to be laid to rest, and the hungry ghost needs to be returned to the land of the dead."

"Okay, so there we have it." I make my tone forcefully

cheerful. "We head over to Europe, find one of the guardians there, and make our way to the underworld. Done deal. Easy peasy lemon squeasy."

Of course it doesn't go like that. Rather more like difficult, difficult, lemon difficult.

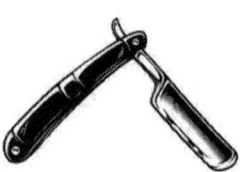

14

Sarroch makes a decent attempt at changing my mind. I mentioned the mule on steroids before, right? I don't abandon friends in need. Ever. What kind of lousy person would I be if I walked away from him now? I'm not going to cut my losses and run when he's in trouble.

Eventually, he gives up, and we all slowly make our way back to the suspended werecat city. Pragya is only mildly apologetic when she informs us that we need to leave immediately. She is, quite rightly, afraid that Sarroch might lose control again, and if he does so with a werecat youngling within reach, that would be a devastating tragedy. She also fears that the longer Sarroch remains in the werecat realm, the more power he will be feeding the hungry ghost.

But I can also read her own fear in her eyes, and so can Sarroch. I feel sad for him, because although he hides it well, I can tell that being feared like this is hard for him.

I can't fully explain why I'm not more scared of him. I probably should be. That moment when he almost tore me apart was one of the most terrifying things I've experienced.

And yet... I know it wasn't him doing it. Sarroch, in control of himself, would never have done that. I know that in a way that I know water is wet.

"At least let Apiya take a bath before we leave," Sarroch is telling Pragya. "She needs it for her injuries."

Pragya hesitates and then agrees.

It's a long and slow process for us to get back to the wicker basket rooms. Sarroch offers to carry me a couple of times. At first I refuse, but halfway up a set of bamboo steps that seem never-ending, I cave. Sometimes feminism has to take a back seat for practicalities and comfort.

Once Sarroch picks me up, we make it back in no time at all.

Back in our rooms, I grab my backpack, kick off my boots, and duck into the bathroom. It's enormous. I mean genuinely huge—it's bigger than the size of my living room and kitchen combined. What the hell do people need so much space for? Especially when there's hardly any furniture, just a large copper tub full of water by the wicker basket's opening, overlooking the canopy.

I stick a finger in the water to find that it's a perfectly warm temperature. Since I don't detect taps, I imagine that there is some kind of magic involved in filling the tub and keeping it warm.

The water is also cloudy and feels just the tiniest bit viscous to the touch. I really hope there isn't bubble bath, bath salts, or something like that. As amusing as it is to think of powerful Mayak heading out into the Mundane realm for bath salts, right now the idea of lowering my body and all my many, many cuts into water full of bath salts makes me wince in anticipation of just how badly that will sting.

To say nothing of the wound at my shoulder and my

skinned leg. I'm hoping my shoulder wound isn't too bad, since Pragya hasn't offered to get a healer to look at me. It has stopped bleeding so it can't be too deep, right?

In order to take a closer look, I need to take off my clothes, but they're stuck to my body from my sweat and my now congealed blood. Lovely.

I peel each item off gingerly, wishing I was wearing clothing so loose and shapeless I could easily step out of it. Getting my leggings off is a trial. Vanity, thy name is woman and all that.

When I first lower myself into the bath, I can't repress hissing as everything starts to sting like crazy. I yelp when the badly skinned patch of leg is submerged.

"Apiya? Apiya!!" Sarroch's voice is loud on the other side of the *very* flimsy bathroom curtain.

"I'm fine!" I call back. I really don't want him to come in right now. "Taking a bath when covered in cuts isn't on my list of favourites activities, that's all."

But weirdly, once I'm fully submerged, the stinging fades away, replaced instead with a rather pleasant sensation. I sigh and lean back against the tub, looking out over that beautifully mesmerising canopy, the water warm against my body. My bones feel like they are being progressively replaced with tepid milk. Despite everything that has just happened, I feel oddly at peace.

I realise I'm in danger of drifting off, so I sit up. I haven't forgotten that Pragya wants us to leave as soon as possible, and I don't want to take the piss by taking a ridiculously long bath.

I look around for that essential item of bath taking—a bar of soap, or some other form of soap dispenser—but there isn't any. In fact, there is another item that is conspicuously missing from the huge bathroom—towels.

"How the hell do you guys get clean and dry if there is no soap and no towels in your bathrooms?" I call out to Sarroch.

"No need for either of those. Just step out of the bath when you're ready."

I rub my fingers in the water, feeling the viscous texture again. Okay, so maybe there is some kind of cleansing agent in the water, but a towel would still be useful. I suppose I can always use one of the spare t-shirts I've brought.

I step out of the bath slowly, and I'm amazed to notice two things. One, my cuts and various injuries look greatly improved. They're now pink and tight, as if the healing is already well underway.

And two, it's like the water peeled off my body to return to the bath—there isn't so much as a stray drop of water clinging to my skin.

Not only that, but as I glance back at the bath, there isn't any dirt or bits of blood floating on the surface. The water is every bit as pristine as when I entered it, and I'm perfectly clean.

That is one handy bath. Maybe when life eventually gets back to normal, I can see if Sarroch could get something similar set up for me in Panong. That could be dangerous, though. I could very conceivably spend every waking hour lounging in this kind of tub.

15

T he journey back to Sarroch's rental car is far less eventful than on the way over to the werecat's realm. Weirdly, this time I'm barely scared at the jump we have to take to leave.

It's daytime, which makes me blink and wince from the brightness of the light. Sarroch explains that time in the werecat realm works a little differently than in the Mundane world. We've been gone for about twenty four hours, even though the light never changed in the werecat realm. Apparently they don't have days and nights there. Werecats sleep when they feel like it, not according to the hours on a clock.

More importantly, that means the full moon is three nights from now—we haven't got much time left. I quash down a sense of panic. One crisis at a time. Once we've taken care of the hungry ghost, that should hopefully solve the problem of Sarroch taking me as his mate.

And if it doesn't...If it doesn't, I'm running out of options. But there's nothing to be achieved by focusing on that right now.

As we make our way back down the mountain, Sarroch decides it would be best for him to be ahead of me so that if anything happens, I don't have my back to him. I feel bad at his pained expression as he tells me this, but I can't argue with him. The reality is that while he would never hurt me himself, there's no telling what the hungry ghost might do.

He also walks slowly enough that I keep up with him easily, for which I'm grateful.

By the time we reach the car, all the recent events are starting to catch up to me, and I feel exhausted. By the time we reach the hotel, the sun is starting to lower, and I'm running on fumes. I sway on my feet as Sarroch books us two adjoining rooms and shuffle after him up the stairs to the first floor. He opens my door for me, hands me my key, and next thing I know I'm ploughing face down onto my bed, arms and legs spreadeagled.

I wake up in pretty much the same position, having drooled onto the bedcovers. What was that about vanity earlier?

On the plus side, I feel much, much better.

From the pitch black out the window, it's clear I've been sleeping for a few hours. My stomach rumbles, and I also realise I have a raging thirst on.

I knock on the adjoining door that leads to Sarroch's bedroom. "Are you awake?"

I hear the lock turn, and the door opens. Sarroch smiles at me in greeting, although his eyes remain tired and wary. "I rarely sleep full nights."

"Insomnia?"

Sarroch shrugs. "No. Same as within the werecat realm. Sleeping at prescribed times of the day is very much a human thing. We werecats sleep when we're tired, not when it's time to go to bed. I like to spend part of the night awake."

"Well, I hope people in Bhutan share your predilection for late nights. Do you know anywhere we can get food and something to drink at this time of night? I'm starving and I'm in need of a stiff drink."

"Give me a few moments."

Sarroch works some magic with the phone and after a while we are furnished with something called gondo datshi, which is the most incredible scrambled eggs I have ever experienced in my whole life—and not just because I'm starving. It has a lot to do with the fact that there is as much butter and Bhutanese cheese in the scramble as there are eggs. It's served with a small mountain of Himalayan red rice, and I inhale most of it down in record time.

"How are you feeling now that we're back in the Mundane world, by the way?" I ask Sarroch in between mouthfuls. "Can you tell a difference in the hold the hungry ghost has on you?"

"I can, in an odd way. It feels like a weight has been lifted. Like I can be amused by things such as the speed with which you eat, whereas it feels like that kind of thing would just have irritated me back in the werecat realm. It's weird. It makes me mistrust my emotions."

"It does make sense, though, since the hungry ghost sounds like it preys on your positive emotions."

The alcohol that Sarroch was able to get tastes as foul as the food tastes good. It's the kind of stuff you could use to clean pennies, strip paint, remove nail varnish, and get blind drunk on, all from the same bottle.

But vile or not, I knock a shot back, because I need it. It burns all the way into my stomach. I reach out with my glass for another.

"Really?" Sarroch asks. "You must really want that, because it's foul."

"Yep. I do."

By the third, I'm really feeling the effects. We're sitting on the foot of his bed, and I thrust my glass at him so he can pour more paint stripper into it. A pleasant warmth is spreading through my body, and the tension that I've been holding onto ever since Yue's attack melts away.

"Are you sure you haven't had enough?" Sarroch asks.

Replacing the tension is a feeling that has me looking over at him.

"What?" He frowns. "Are you okay?"

It takes me a moment to establish whether I am drunk enough to do what I have in mind. Turns out that yes, I am.

"Apiya?"

I release my glass, which goes rolling on the rug, bouncing without breaking, and I swing myself clumsily over until I'm sitting on Sarroch's lap, straddling him, with my knees bent. He goes very still.

"Apiya, what are you doing?"

I laugh. "Do we need to have the talk about the birds and the bees and what happens between a man and a woman?"

"This is a bad idea."

"Probably," I agree cheerfully. "But that's never stopped me before."

"You're drunk. I'm not taking advantage of you when you're drunk."

"Ah, but see, you're not taking advantage. *I'm* taking advantage of my own drunkenness to do something I probably wouldn't have the courage to do if I was sober."

"Sometimes I really don't get you. I showed myself to be an actual monster, the kind of monster people were afraid I might be, and not only do you not run a mile, you..."

"Straddle you in a hotel room. Hmm-hmm. That's just

how I roll." I giggle. For some reason, that thought strikes me as highly funny.

"It's not funny." Although he doesn't quite manage to stop a smile tugging at his lips. "Why are you laughing?" His smile widens as I fall into properly helpless laughter.

By the time I stop laughing, I realise that his hands have crept around to hold onto my hips, his fingers digging into my skin with just the right amount of intensity.

Hello, sailor.

"I think this is a bad idea," he repeats. "I'm serious, Apiya."

"I agree. The removal of clothes is a very serious business." I focus my attention, and with clumsy fingers, I fumble with his shirt's top button.

He grabs my hands gently with one of his to stop me. His other hand is still at my hip, though. "What if I hurt you?"

"Ah, but you forget my superpower." I let a hint of silver reach the surface of my left hand and Sarroch winces, releasing it at once. "And anyway, it will be fine..." the last word is cut off by a hiccup. I giggle again.

"And what if it's not? There's no rush. We should wait for another time. A time when this is sorted."

"That's a terrible idea. Unless you don't want to..."

"No, I want to. I really do." The slight strain in his voice has my stomach doing a very happy flip. "I just *really* don't want to hurt you again. That would kill me. And I don't feel right about this."

I grab both of his shoulders. "Sarroch, I've not turned into a porcelain doll all of a sudden."

"No, but I *have* turned into a monster." He looks away from me.

I grab his chin with one hand and bring him back to face me. "Then you can be my monster. I've always wanted one."

Before he can repeat his protests of being serious and this being a bad idea, I kiss him. I feel him jolt from the surprise of it, and then both his arms snake around me, crushing me close.

"No, wait." He pushes me back a little. We're both a little breathless. "I don't know how you can trust me when even I don't trust myself anymore."

"It's because...because...I need this." The words blurt themselves out of my mouth as if someone else has spoken them. "I need this," I repeat, realising how much it's true. I'm no longer joking at all. "Everything that's happened of late —Yue nearly killed me, Chizu nearly killed me, I killed Chizu, I was nearly executed by the Mayak... And then what happened back in the werecat realm. I came so close to being completely destroyed. And I just... I need to feel alive. I really need to feel *alive*." Suddenly I don't feel as drunk any more.

"And you need this too," I whisper. "I need this to feel alive, and you need this to not feel like a monster."

The words actually bring tears stinging just behind my eyes. I'm not sure why this suddenly matters so much to me, I just know that it really does. This is important, desperately important.

I already live with death inside me, because to save me, Mr Sangong infused my energy into a dead human newborn. Through some magical process, I'm now alive, even though I will always carry death inside me.

And coming so very close to destruction, I need to feel fully alive again. I need that reassurance.

Sarroch is holding on to my hips so tightly now his fingers are almost hurting me, digging into my flesh. One quick look at his face is all I need to know, just how right I was about him. The naked vulnerability I see in his eyes is almost overwhelming.

I hold his gaze, my fingers returning to his shirt buttons. This time they're less clumsy, as if the intensity of the moment burnt through the alcohol.

I get them undone and push the shirt off his shoulders. He helps to shrug it off, his eyes never leaving mine. It's like I have him hypnotised, and the feeling is heady.

I break away from his gaze, looking down as I run my hands over his skin. It's smooth and warm and feels like silk under my fingers.

I've seen him naked before, of course, but I wasn't really free to notice. And now that I am—*damn* if he doesn't look good without a shirt.

I look back up at him. His eyes are half-lidded now, languorous.

"Well, fair's fair." He grabs the bottom of my t-shirt and lifts it up above my head. I laugh as I stretch my arms up to help him along.

He brings his hands to rest at my waist again, and we look at each other for a long moment.

And then his hands are framing my face and mine are digging into his hair and our mouths are crushed against each other, need pumping like heat from his body to mine, and back to his.

He groans and grabs me, spinning me around and throwing me back on the bed so I'm beneath him.

My head is spinning dizzy, dancing circles. Every sensation is bursting through my nerves, the taste of him, the hard planes of him, the springiness of the mattress beneath me, the flutter of the fan against my bare skin.

He takes me with quick, hard hands and restless lips, and I hold on to him with greedy hands, getting just what I wanted—something raw and primal and so very, very much alive.

———

I WAKE UP WITH THE MORNING LIGHT. IT'S NICE HAVING sunrises and sunsets again. As nice as our short stint in the werecat realm was, I prefer this world. It takes me a few blinks to remember where I am. I turn over to be greeted by a smile from Sarroch.

"Morning," I mumble, rubbing a hand over my eyes.

He pushes himself up and kisses me on the temple. "Good morning."

I feel weirdly shy all of a sudden. Last night was pretty incredible. Very incredible.

"We need to get up," he says. "Make sure we catch the plane to London." He looks apologetic. "I've done a lot of thinking while you were sleeping, and our best bet to reach the underworld will be Charon, the ferryman across the River Styx. These days he's based in London."

I sit up at once, now feeling wide awake. "Absolutely. I'll jump in the shower, throw some clothes on, and then I'll be ready."

I'm still feeling all warm and happy as we arrive at Paro Airport. But as we step out onto the airstrip, that warm happiness evaporates like piss hitting an overheated plane engine.

"No way. You have got to be bloody kidding me." I turn to look at Sarroch, almost too incredulous for words.

The rust bucket is back. Or I should say is still here.

"You seriously expect me to fly all the way to *London* in that? No way, Sarroch. No *way*. I will stand by you while an evil hungry ghost takes you over like some kind of demented poltergeist, but I am *not* flying all the way to London in that death trap."

Sarroch smiles. "It's only to go to Kathmandu. From there, we'll take a commercial plane. A very modern Boeing – I checked, and they assured me that there are all kinds of digital screens in the cockpit. There are so few flights in and out of Paro, I couldn't book us something where the timings work to catch our flight to London from Kathmandu."

"A Boeing?" I ask suspiciously.

"A Boeing."

"How many digital screens does it have?"

"*Lots*. And things that beep, and a radar. It's a regular commercial flight." As he speaks, Sarroch ushers me towards the plane, and I follow with all the reticence of a house cat being led to the bath. "And you'll be pleased to hear that I won't be piloting the Boeing, either. We will be sitting in regular seats, and I will make sure there's champagne for takeoff. No luxury spared."

"I bloody well hope so after I have to fly again in that *thing*." My stomach is already cramping in anticipation of the ordeal that awaits.

As we reach the plane, I stop. "Can we make a deal? I help you sort out this hungry ghost thing, and you bring me back here? To Bhutan. I want to come back to Paro and get to know it better. And Bhutan in general. I think I would like it here."

"Apiya, if we're able to get this sorted, you can have whatever you want and go wherever you want."

I raise an eyebrow at him. "Careful with those kinds of statements. I will hold you to them."

Sarroch smiles "Done." His face turns serious. "Seriously. I won't ever forget this, Apiya. There aren't many people who would stand by me after what I did back there."

"There's a reason the insanity plea is a real thing in the Mundane world. You can't be held responsible if somebody else controls your actions. And I *know* you, Sarroch. You've got a lot of flaws, mister, but you're not a monster."

My hand's on the handrail of the stairs leading up to the death-and-gravity-defying, bone-shaking bucket of rusted bolts. Sarroch's hand covers mine.

"You really are one in a million, Apiya."

"I am indeed."

He leans towards me. I'm expecting a sizzling kiss, something reminiscent of last night. Instead, he shucks me under the chin. "And don't think I haven't noticed you're stalling getting on the plane."

I snort with laughter. "Well spotted." I glance up at the rust bucket. "I can't believe I'm putting myself through that again." I take a step up the stairs and every cell in my body starts screaming at me to return to the solid tarmac. "What does it say about your plane that I'm more scared of being in it than of being with you?"

"I think it says very little about my plane, and a lot about you," Sarroch replies.

Touché.

16

We make it to Kathmandu without any issues and from there transfer into a beautifully, blessedly modern plane. I have never been so appreciative of commercial airlines before, but they truly are a thing of beauty.

After a smooth, rattle-and-lurch-free flight, we land at Heathrow Airport. The plane doesn't bounce down the runway while simultaneously trying to shake itself to pieces. In fact, the landing is so smooth I sleep through it, right up until the captain welcomes us to England.

I will never take modern aviation for granted ever again.

After disembarking, we're making our way through immigration, this time travelling like two regular people. It means queuing with the rest of the Mundanes rather than getting any special welcome like we'd received in Bhutan.

There are machines ahead that scan passports and faces, but they malfunction half of the time, so the queue crawls slowly forward. Any time I'm stuck in a queue I get the urge to moo as a joke, which to me seems hilarious, but people rarely get it.

I'm debating whether Sarroch is ready to meet the dorkier side of my sense of humour when his mobile beeps. He checks it and curses.

I sigh. "Why do I detect a problem?" Can we not get *anything* to go right on this trip?

"A message from my assistant. She was supposed to book us a car but evidently some of our European compatriots were paying close enough attention to notice what she was doing."

"Paying attention how?"

"They're more enmeshed in Mundane government out here, and they sometimes keep tabs on things like when my UK accounts spend in Europe to monitor my whereabouts. It's been a while since they've done that, so I thought we'd be in the clear. Well, if I'm honest, I was so preoccupied with everything I didn't think to tell my assistant to use a non-European account to pay for the car."

"Why would they care if you're here, though?"

"It's a territory thing. We can't have anyone know I'm in London—it will create diplomacy issues which will make their way back to the Mayak Elders. And even if it doesn't create issues, the Mayak Elders have enough plants in London that they will find out."

"Right, and that will lead them to question why we're here, which might lead them to discovering your hungry ghost problem, which then means they'll know we—well, *I* lied about you having chosen me as your mate."

Sarroch gives me a penetrating look. "It's not a lie any longer. It's just missing a technicality."

The immigration guy waves me over to a passport scanning machine before I have time to ask if that means Sarroch's tiger is changing how he feels about me. For some reason, that thought makes me blush, as if I were a teenage girl with a crush.

I get through passport control and wait for him on the other side. I'll rent us a car, and then we can keep things discreet. No one will know about me, so they won't be looking out for me. I whip out my phone to look up reviews and rates for rental cars at the airport—and more importantly, to find the cheapest one as car rental in England is expensive.

"Api!!" a voice squeals before I can do anything more than type 'car rental Heathrow Airport' into Google.

I look up just in time to catch a multicolour blur crashing into me and squeezing me into oblivion.

"Oh my *god*, Api, I can't believe you're *here*!"

Once my shock dissipates enough for my brain to work again, I recognise Priscilla, my oldest friend. "Pree! What... What are you doing here?"

She releases me and steps back. "Oh, you know me. Can't have money burning a hole in my pocket for too long. I had a bit of cash from my latest job, so I quit and took myself off to Greece. Now I'm back to not having two pennies together—the way nature intended." She's grinning as she speaks.

I suppose you could technically say that Pree's a tall, leggy blonde, because she's all those things, but that is so very far from who she is. It would be like describing a peacock as simply a bird to someone who has never seen a peacock before.

Technically correct, but vastly inadequate to capture all that a peacock *is*.

Pree is dressed in a style only Pree can pull off. Over the knee purple and black striped socks. A pair of hot pants covered in a pattern of Liquorice All Sorts. At least three or maybe even four belts—it's hard to count them because they all overlap each other—are looped around her slender hips, some of them little more than long pieces of chain. A cone bra reminiscent of the one Madonna wore in her Blonde Ambition tour, under a top made of very loose black mesh. Calling it a top is generous since it only reaches about a few inches below her bra, leaving her washboard stomach and outie belly button exposed. Over her top is an open tweed waistcoat. Her shoes are the same as she wore when we were teenagers together—beat up, maroon Doc Martens that reach up to just below her knees.

Like I said, her style is distinctive and very uniquely hers. Pree was a beanpole when we were teenagers. She's still taller than me now, with barely more curves than she had back then, but she's got a lot more muscle tone. Her skin is pale to the point of milkiness and she would be a natural blonde if she didn't dye her hair.

"You look *fab*, Api. It's really so good to see you. And look at your hair." She touches it, giving a dramatic sigh. "I've missed having you around to sort my hair out. It's just a disaster at the moment."

I eye Pree's locks. Disaster's a fair description. Vomit green is a nasty colour, generally speaking, but it's especially bad for someone of her colouring. "I can't disagree with you there. What the hell happened?"

"Last dye job turned to this colour, not the teal I was after. I could either go in search of better quality dye and forgo a couple of cocktails in Greece, or I could say 'sod it' and spank *all* my money on a holiday."

I grin. "Let's face it, 'sod it' is your mantra in life."

"True, that." She rubs a hand over the left side of her head, which is now shaved. The rest of her hair is long and thick, falling in waves over her right shoulder and down her back. She has beautiful hair—when she doesn't screw it up with bad dye jobs.

I used to envy it when I was young, running my fingers through it when I plaited it for her. I envied the waves, because my own hair was and still is ramrod straight. I got over it, of course, but there was a time when I would have killed for Pree's hair.

"I shaved the side of my head to make up for the bad dye job," Pree continues. "I kind of like it."

"I do too. It suits you." And it really does. Her features are fine, almost elfin, and the bare side of her head emphasises them.

Sarroch reaches my side, having finished his struggle with the passport scanning immigration machine. "Is everything okay?"

"Yeah. I just bumped into an old friend. This is—"

Pree sticks her hand out at him. "Priscilla. Like the queen of the desert." She raises an eyebrow at him. "Your eyes look like they're about to bug out of your head."

"Forgive me," Sarroch replies dryly. "I don't normally see people in airports in their underwear."

"Underwear?" she hoots in reply. "That's called fashion —dah-ling. What kind of repressed Victorian era women are you used to back in Asia? At least that answers the question of whether you're shagging Api, since I know she wouldn't poke up with that kind of attitude."

Sarroch looks out-of-this-world awkward, and Pree laughs. "Ohh, no, I got it wrong! You *are* shagging Api. Well *done*, mate." She slaps him on the arm. "You've got excellent taste." She threads an arm through mine and tugs me towards baggage reclaim before he can formulate a response. "Glad we got that cleared up, or I would have made a pass at your man. He's *hot*. Well done you. And he looks expensive." She sighs. "I could *so* use a wealthy man since I'm flat out broke after my Greece trip. So, how come you're back in London?"

"I'm here to help Sarroch tend to some business." I keep things vague on purpose.

Although Pree knows about my magic, I never told her about the Mayak or any of the supernaturals who live in London. It's not that I don't trust her—on the contrary, I trust her completely. Well, that is, I trust her to keep secrets, and I'd trust her to have my back. That kind of thing.

What I don't trust is for her to not put herself in danger. I've never met someone as fearless as she is. That might sound like a compliment, and in a way it is, but it also means she tends to act like she has no concept of safety, no filter or self-preservation instinct to stop her from doing stupid things or go ploughing headlong into bad situations.

When we were young, this made her a lot of fun. She was always attempting new tricks on the dirt bike track, for example, and she would come up with these crazy ideas that she would then drag me along for. We got into trouble on several occasions, and as we got older, I started to rein her in a bit, kind of acting like the sensible and cautious one.

Trouble in the world of Mundanes is one thing. Trouble in the supernatural world is something else entirely. When I realised I was going to leave England to go to Panong to find others with magic like me, I was genuinely afraid that if I told Pree that London has its own magical society, she'd go charging in, looking for it.

That's a great way to get killed and in short order, and I wouldn't have been there to look out for her. So I'd kept it all to myself, making up another reason to explain my move.

I feel bad about doing that, I really do. But I'd feel way

worse if Pree got entangled with deadly magical predators because of me.

"What business? Where are you going?" Pree asks.

"Good old London town, actually. We're going to go rent a car, and—"

"You'll do no such thing. I left my car in the long-term car park. Consider me your own private chauffeur. Do you have suitcases to pick up first?"

"No, we travelled light. But Pree—"

"Great. I only have hand luggage as well." Which is a remarkably small backpack, considering her love of clothes. "All you need for a holiday to Greece is a bikini and a sarong." She winks at Sarroch.

"I'm a fan of travelling light also, obviously." Sarroch seems to be getting over his initial shock, graduating to amusement. "But I think it would be best if we just rented a car all the same."

Pree considers him. "What kind of 'business' are you into, anyway?"

"The discrete kind."

Pree stops abruptly and narrows her eyes at him. "If you're into drugs or anything else illegal...I swear if you've got Api caught up in something dodgy—"

"It's nothing like that," I hasten to reassure her, before some airport security person overhears her.

"Well then, what is it like?" Pree eyes Sarroch, still obviously suspicious. I think every member of her family has done prison at some point or another, so that's why she's quick to jump to that kind of conclusion.

I shift awkwardly. I hate having to lie to her. I'm crap at it at the best of times, but doing it when I'm unprepared, and in front of someone I truly care about, well, that's even worse.

"He's got magic too, hasn't he?" she says abruptly.

Sarroch shoots me a worried look. We're in a busy airport terminal with lots of people walking about, and even without making a scene, Pree attracts a hell of a lot of attention. Everyone is glancing at her as they walk past us.

The last thing we need is to be getting into a lengthy discussion about all things magical right now, especially with people within earshot.

I make a decision. At this point, damage control is best, and that means containing the situation. "Okay, let's go to your car. We would be really grateful if you could give us a lift. Thanks, Pree."

She smiles widely. "Glad to hear it." She threads her arm through mine again, walking briskly, her long legs taking wide strides as she drags me along towards the exit.

It feels like being a teenager all over again, down to that sinking feeling in my stomach that Pree is about to get me into some kind of trouble.

17

"Are you sure this is a good idea?" Sarroch asks me as we wait for Pree to pay the parking fee for her car. I'll give her money to contribute to it later. She won't have been exaggerating when she said she's broke. She's the absolute worst at managing money.

"Not at all, but I know her. She wouldn't have given up, and that kind of attention is bad for us right now, especially somewhere like a busy airport terminal. And it does solve the problem of anyone knowing you're in town. I can't imagine people would expect you to be travelling with someone like Pree."

"You can say that again. And she doesn't know about magic?"

"She knows about mine, and I'm not sure how much more she's put together over the years." I explain about my fear that she'd likely go enthusiastically charging after London's supernatural society, because it would be 'a fun adventure' or 'just because it's fascinating'.

Sarroch winces. "In that case, I agree with your decision

to keep her in the dark. Doing that would most likely end extremely badly."

Pree returns to our side. "Okay, all done. My car's this way." She points, and we all head off. "So, tell me how long you two have been seeing each other? I need to know all the details so I can decide whether or not to bestow the 'child-hood friend' stamp of approval."

I take pity on Sarroch, who's looking awkward, probably because we technically only got together after what happened in the werecat realm, and that's not a story he's going to want people to know. Nor do I, really, because I don't want people misjudging him. "I'll tell you all about it another day, Pree. Maybe when this business is taken care of, you and I can go out for a drink."

"Done deal. And then can you do your magic with my hair as a thank you for my driving services today?"

"I wouldn't dream of leaving London until your hair is a colour that doesn't make my plane meal want to come back for a revisit."

"I wouldn't mind purple," Pree muses.

I smile. "That was your favourite colour growing up."

"Still is. I wanted a change—goes to show what a stupid idea *that* was."

We walk out into the car park. A fine drizzle is falling. Ah, England in August. The month that in most of the Northern Hemisphere conjures up images of warm, sun-filled afternoons, barbecues in the park, and cocktails on the beach.

Not in England. It's damp and slightly chilly, because obviously the three days of summer are already done, and autumn has decided to get a head start. I'm so glad of my fleece.

And of course it helps that it hides all my various cuts

and injuries. It'd be awkward to introduce the new man in my life covered in injuries. Things are complicated enough as it is.

We reach Pree's car, and Sarroch raises an eyebrow at me.

"And you gave me a hard time over the state of my plane?"

"Your plane?" Pree echoes, her eyebrows shooting up towards her hair.

"It's a rust bucket," I reply.

"A plane is a plane is a plane." Pree turns to Sarroch. "You have a *plane*? That is an *excellent* way to get the best friend seal of approval. All the more so if you offer to take me for a ride in it."

"Easy," I counter. "Sarroch's plane is *not* worth your stamp of approval. As far as planes go, it's more crappy than your car. He'll get the seal of approval *in spite* of the plane."

"It has character," Sarroch protests.

"So does my car." Pree grins at him over the car, unlocking it. "If Api screws things up, feel free to look me up. I, for one, wouldn't be so ungrateful as to protest over having a private plane."

"Oi!" I protest, laughing as I climb into the car. I'm well aware that Pree's joking. She's mental in many ways, but she's more loyal than a golden retriever. Sarroch will now be of as much interest to her as a relative, but she does like to joke around.

Sarroch crams himself in the back. "I'm very happy with Apiya," he says awkwardly. I'll need to tell him later that Pree's humour is like her clothes. An acquired taste.

It's a bit early in...well whatever our relationship is at this point...for him to be meeting important people in my life, and to start with Pree is definitely a dive into the deep end.

"Course you are happy with Api, sunshine," Pree replies. "She's the best girl in the world. You'd have to be deaf, blind, and a moron of the highest degree not to be happy with her." She leans across the gear stick, grabs me, and smacks me a kiss on the cheek. "It's good to have you back in Blighty."

Yeah, it really is like being a teenager again, when it seemed to me that Pree was the most wonderful, most awesome, most amazing person I'd ever met.

————

PREE'S CAR IS A PROPER TURD ON WHEELS. I'M NOT BEING mean to Pree. I'd happily tell her that to her face, and she'd readily agree. I know this because she was the one who cheerfully announced that she had acquired a turd on wheels back when she bought the car. And that was a long time ago.

It's an Austin Allegro, which is a small, boxy, ugly car with a crap engine. The colour is supposed to be mustard yellow, but it looks like mustard yellow that got mixed with bird poo. Inside, the seats are upholstered in this horrid, slightly textured brown fabric, like a rough version of synthetic velour.

The car's bodywork is covered in dents and scratches, and the middle of the bonnet is being eaten by rust. Pree turns on the engine, and it coughs, wheezes, and emits a disturbing blue smoke from its exhaust.

As he tries to get comfortable in the back, Sarroch's feet crinkle wrappers and dislodge a few empty bottles and cans. "You, er...have a lot of stuff back here."

"Ah, yeah. Sorry. I'm a bit of a messy bugger. Didn't expect to have company." Pree doesn't look embarrassed in the least.

The first time I went to her house as a kid, it was such a trial. Her room was the messiest I'd ever seen. I tried, but I couldn't hack it. I had to tidy it for her, while Pree looked on, finding the whole thing hilarious. She wasn't embarrassed about the state of her room, nor did she take offence at me tidying for her. It took me a while before I could be relaxed enough at her place to not clean and tidy the whole time I was there.

The car crawls forward. "I can't go above fifty miles per hour or it overheats," Pree explains. "Where are we going, by the way?"

"Hammersmith," Sarroch replies.

I turn around in my seat to face him. "Hammersmith? Really?" That is *not* where I'd expect Charon, ferryman of souls, to be living. Hammersmith is nondescript. It's just a regular residential neighbourhood. It's not the suburbs, but it's not Camden, or Shoreditch, or Dalston—or any of the cooler neighbourhoods. Hammersmith is where families with two point four children live.

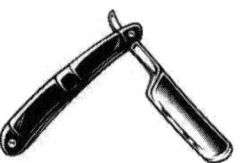

18

We make quite the arrival as we pull up into a small, anonymous carpark in Hammersmith, Pree's car crawling to a wheezing, juddering stop. The sun is setting, and the jet lag is tugging more and more insistently at my eyelids. I can't stop yawning. A quick check in the mirror confirms that I now look bleary-eyed.

Sarroch, on the other hand, looks fresher than a daisy just plucked from the field. Which is to be expected for a magical being.

On the positive side of things, the drizzle has stopped.

Pree turns in her seat to face Sarroch. "So, truth time. You have magic, don't you?"

Sarroch shoots me a questioning glance.

"Don't look at Apiya. I know you do. I'm not stupid."

"Nobody thinks you are," I reply, not wanting her to feel hurt that I didn't tell her the full story about just how much magic there is in London, to say nothing of the world.

"I know you've kept a lot of stuff from me. It's why we've kind of lost touch these last few years, isn't it?"

I can't meet her eye. She's right, though. Because I

couldn't tell her the truth about my life in Panong, calling her to catch up grew increasingly awkward, which meant we didn't quite drift apart, but we stopped speaking as often. It seemed like the right thing to do at the time, like I was looking out for her in spite of her, but now I feel horridly guilty.

"I'm not upset," Pree says. "A bit confused as to why you wouldn't tell me what was going on, though. I know you trust me, so what gives?"

I grimace. "It's just such a dangerous world. I was worried you'd go charging in..." That just sounds worse. Patronising. I'm realising that it wasn't really my business trying to decide for her whether she could or couldn't have any involvement with the magical world.

"Yeah, because I do always go charging in." Pree's tone is level, neutral. "It's a fair assumption that I'd do that. But it's my life, Api. It's for me to decide what risks I take or not. You can't wrap me in cotton wool without my consent."

"I know. I'm really sorry, Pree. I thought I was doing the right thing...You know I wouldn't do anything to hurt you."

"I know. That's why I'm not upset. And I'll forgive all if you tell me what kind of magic Sarroch has."

I turn back to shoot a questioning look at Sarroch. He nods.

"Wait, wait, wait, let me try to guess," Pree says eagerly. "You're a...wizard."

He gives an impatient snort. "Do I really look that weak? I'm not playing the game if *that* is your first guess."

"Wizards are weak?" Pree's eyes are sparkling.

"Compared to a weretiger as old as me? Yes, they are."

"A weretiger? Like a werewolf, but a tiger? *Cool!*" She gives me a sly look. "And a weretiger is quite the upgrade from Stephen Weatherbough."

"Who's that?" Sarroch asks as we all climb out of the car.

"Apiya's boyfriend for a fleeting few weeks at school, and a total waste of space," Pree replies.

"He wasn't a total waste of space," I grumble, not because it's not true, but because I'm still a tad embarrassed that I fell for someone who really *was* a total waste of space.

"He was ninety-nine percent a waste of space," Pree confirms cheerfully. "Sarroch, I thought you were all right before, but knowing you're a weretiger, you *totally* get my seal of approval."

"Well, thank you."

"So what now?" she asks.

"Now, we thank you for the lift and make plans to meet up with you when we're done," Sarroch replies.

"No way. You think I'm going to miss out on seeing magic in action?"

There you go. That's why I kept the truth from her.

"This isn't a matter of seeing magic in action," Sarroch replies. "It's a matter of things being too dangerous to have a human involved."

"Api's human, and I'm not letting her walk into danger without a friend at her back."

"I have her back," Sarroch growls.

"Not if you're busy tending to your 'business'," she replies.

"Pree, much as I appreciate it, he's right," I interrupt. "This isn't something for a human to get involved with."

"*You're* human."

Actually, I'm not really, but I'm not ready to get into all of that. "I have magic."

"And I have this."

She walks over to the back of the car and pops the boot —wait, let me rephrase that. She unlocks the boot, which creaks open with all the musical charm of an old door in a horror movie. She reaches in.

"A cricket bat?" Sarroch asks.

"For protection. Very effective." She pats it then slams the trunk shut with a shriek of tortured metal. "No one bothers me when I have it."

"No one *human*," I point out.

"Well, if the magical creatures of London have bothered me, I either took care of them, or they decided to leave me alone on account of the bat. So, where are we going?"

I look at Sarroch. "I don't know that we'll win this argument."

"Oh, yes we will." He turns to face her, and his eyes grow large and dark, two deep inkwells. He's going to hypnotise her, or whatever it is he does when he does that mind control thing. "You will stay here," he tells Pree, his voice deeper than normal. Gold flecks swim deep in his irises.

Pree lifts her bat and rests it against her shoulder. "Nope, I'm coming with you."

Sarroch looks confused. He tries again, telling her to get back into the car, and again she says no. I reach out—I can feel his magic rolling off him, but it seems to then slide off Pree, like water down a window.

"Does she have magic?" he asks me. "If she does, I can't sense it."

"Nor can I."

Now it's Pree's turn to look confused. "What's the matter?"

"Sarroch should have hypnotised you into doing what he wants." I reach out to her again, but all I can feel is her, her energy, nothing remotely magical. All the same, it's properly weird that Sarroch couldn't control her with his magic.

"I'm not the best at compelling," Sarroch says, "But I definitely have enough to control a Mundane."

Pree shrugs. "I don't believe in hypnosis, if that helps." She grins. "And I'm anything but 'mundane'. So I guess that means I'm coming with you. Where to?"

"I would really rather you didn't come," Sarroch replies.

She shrugs and continues to look at him expectantly.

Sarroch sighs. "Fine. But if things get dangerous or scary, don't get in the way."

"I have my bat."

Sarroch shakes his head. "And I hope you don't have to realise just how useless it is."

"Whatever you say. So? What's the deal?"

"We're going to look for Charon, the ferryman for the dead. Can you handle that?"

"Can I just! Where do we find him, this ferryman?"

"He lives down at the river front, on a houseboat."

"Houseboat. Got it. Wait, I read about the river Styx during my trip to Greece. Isn't Charon the ferryman from there?"

"The river Styx is any body of water, and these days, Charon has chosen to base himself in Hammersmith. Who knows why?"

"Right. Houseboats it is." Even for Pree, that is an impressive level of unflappability, having just discovered about weretigers, ferrymen for the dead, and the River Styx being real.

She turns back to me. "See, this is better than keeping it all a secret. And I might be of help." She frowns. "Api, you look terrible, you know that? Sarroch's magic is obviously way more potent than yours, because he's not showing any signs of jet lag."

"Thanks, Captain Obvious," I reply, my tone sarcastic.

Sarroch reaches from behind me to knead my shoulders. "If we had the time to rest up, I'd suggest we do that," he says apologetically. "But the full moon is tomorrow night. We're getting tight on time."

We all start to walk towards the river.

"As hot as having a supernatural boyfriend is, I think going for the regular mortal is probably better for the self-esteem," Pree announces. "It would do my nut in to be with someone who always looks so perfect all the time."

"Somehow this doesn't feel like a compliment to me," I reply, amused.

Sarroch turns to her. "Do you always say whatever thoughts come into your head?"

"Pretty much."

"Yeah, she doesn't have a filter," I confirm. "You get used to it. It's part of her charm."

"As is this." Pree swings her bat down, and then back across her shoulders. She continues towards the river at a brisk pace.

Sarroch and I follow her. "Does the way I look bother you?" he asks me in a low voice.

I smile and slip my hand in his. "You have many flaws, Sarroch. Including your taste in planes. And you come with more baggage than a plane full of holiday goers. But the one thing you do have going for you is that you always look like you just stepped out of a magazine, which I like. I like having pretty things to look at."

Sarroch laughs. "The *one* thing I have going for me?"

I grin. "What can I say? I'm shallow like that."

"I don't think anyone's called me pretty before."

"As we established earlier, I'm one in a million."

"All right, you two lovebirds," Pree calls. "No need to make me nauseous with your public displays of affections.

Remember that you're in England. Land of repressed emotions, stifled sexuality, and most importantly, the place where the closest we get to expressing affection for someone is to call them a silly bugger."

Sarroch leans down to me. "I'm guessing last night came courtesy of your Panongian heritage, then."

I wink at him, but we unlink hands as we reach the waterfront, not because of what Pree said, but because this genuinely is serious business.

19

The river is placid, the water a dark, murky brown that's rapidly turning to black. To our left, the dark green and gold Hammersmith Bridge crosses the river, the last remnants of sunlight catching on the gold accents. The actual river front has a pedestrian walkway along which are various pubs, music and voices spilling out from the open doors and windows.

A number of barges—houseboats—are docked three or four deep, so that the owners of the ones furthest away will have to step across their neighbours' boats to get to shore. Something that strikes me as quite cosy—boat people must have quite the tight-knit community.

Some of the boats look like they've been here for decades, more like permanent fixtures than methods of transportation. Some have little potted plants and well-maintained paint, looking so pretty and neat they could be featured in some of those interior decoration magazines. While yet others look like they are owned by crusty hippies or hermits—shabby, run down, and I smell weed wafting out through more than one window covered by tie-dyed fabric.

"So, where do we find Charon?" I ask Sarroch.

"I'll be able to sense him."

We walk along the waterfront, Sarroch peering out at the boats. As ever when Pree is involved, we attract looks, but she's utterly unbothered. I'm pretty impervious to what people think of me, but Pree is on a whole other level. She's like Teflon. Nothing sticks. She does what she does, she is who she is, and what people think isn't even a distant blip on her radar.

We reach the end of the houseboats. "He's not in the boats," Sarroch says.

"The pubs?" Pree suggests.

"Yes, most likely."

We turn back, popping in and out of each pub long enough for Sarroch to scan each one.

I've seen what guardians of the underworld look like in Asia. Berata Kala is a fearsome sight. Charon looks human, so he won't need to hide his form, but I'm still expecting a man with a certain gravitas.

Sarroch finds him standing outside of a pub, having a smoke with a couple other men. "Charon? We need to have a word with you."

"What did he call you?" one of the men ask him.

Charon glares at Sarroch. "A nickname from childhood. Give me a second, boys." He steps away, not looking happy.

He has the hard, round belly of a man who enjoys more than just a pint of an evening. His trousers ride low, held in place beneath the swell of his belly by a brown leather belt. His shirt front reaches for, but doesn't quite manage to stay tucked into his trousers, peeking out of the bottom of a shapeless jumper. A flat cap completes the look.

He must be altering his human form—there's no way the real Charon actually looks like this. It's effective camouflage. He blends in far better than those Mayak who go for the ultra beautiful look, like Yue.

"I don't like being disturbed when among Mundanes," he hisses at Sarroch once we're far enough from the men to be out of earshot. His voice sounds completely different from what he used when he was talking with his friends. I can hear it through my ears as well as inside my head, and it has an impossible echo given that we are out in the open.

An electric shiver runs down my spine, that buzzing feeling I get when I'm in the presence of strong magic.

"And what are you doing here, anyway?" Charon asks Sarroch. He leans over to put his pint down on the ground, then pulls out a packet of cigarettes and lights one.

"Nice plumber's crack," Pree tells him. "Now I finally understand why so many builders are afflicted by this ailment—clearly it's so serious not even magic can fix it."

Whatever magic Charon has, it's clear Pree can't feel it.

"Not the time," Sarroch snaps at her, his voice hard. Pree nods at once, looking apologetic.

Sarroch turns to the ferryman. "Charon, I need to ask for your services tonight."

Charon takes a hit of his cigarette. "Services, is it?" Now he sounds entirely like a normal Londoner. From South London, in fact.

"I need to cross over," Sarroch says.

"And why would you want to do that?"

"I have unfinished business that I should have dealt with a long time ago."

Charon shrugs. "So does everyone. Get yourself a proper permit through the official channels, and I'll gladly take you across."

"My business is...discreet."

"You and everyone else's. No one likes to air their dirty laundry out in public, and unfinished business with the dead is always dirty business..." Charon is turning away from Sarroch when his eyes catch mine and he pauses.

"What?" I ask. I realise with an unpleasant shock that his eyes are of mismatched colour. One is a pale green, almost like jade, the other is dark enough to look black in the slowly settling night.

It's not the fact that the colour is mismatched that bothers me, per se. In fact, I'm not sure why I'm feeling this uncomfortable under his gaze, and yet I can't look away.

"And why are they here?" he asks, obviously referring to Pree and I, although he's just looking at me.

"I'm here to help Sarroch," I reply, pushing past my discomfort. "Pree won't be crossing."

Charon takes another drag on his cigarette. The tip glows in the settling night, reflecting in his eyes. "It's been a while since I took a live human across."

"The girls are staying right here," Sarroch says suddenly. "I'm going alone.".

"Hang on, I came here to help you," I protest.

"It's not safe. I don't know what I was thinking—a temporary moment of stupidity on my part. I'm going alone. This is my business and I can't be putting you in that kind of danger."

"I'm perfectly capable of deciding what level of danger I'm prepared to take on," I snap, a little bit more curtly than I'd intended.

"Totally see where you're coming from," Pree says. "Isn't it annoying when somebody else tries to decide what is safe for you and what isn't?"

I glare at her. "Really not the time."

Charon is looking at Sarroch, his expression having changed from stony to interested. "You don't want them to cross?"

"No."

"Then that is my price. If you want to cross without going through the official channels, all three of you have to come."

"What? Why?"

Charon's mismatched eyes glitter dangerously, the pale green iris seems to swirl as if it's some kind of vortex or something. "You have come to London without our permission," he tells Sarroch in that soft voice that somehow echoes. "You know you are breaking quite a few agreements by simply being here and asking me to take you across. You do not get to negotiate or question me. You don't want the humans to cross, so they will cross. Your unease will be my price."

Sarroch's own face darkens. I smell ozone in the air, and the pressure and battery licking feeling against my skin intensifies.

"Step back," I whisper to Pree.

"Huh? Why?"

"You can't feel anything?"

She shakes her head. I mutter a curse under my breath. If she can't feel that level of magic, then having her around could be more dangerous than I thought—she'll have no warning of incoming danger.

As rapidly as it built up, the pressure and smell of ozone disappear.

"You're right," Sarroch says. "I apologise for being out of line just now. This unfinished business is... Weighing heavily on me. Part of the reason I want to take care of it is because it is having far too much of an influence on me and my behaviour." His tone is polite, now. Formal. "Maybe we can come to some kind of arrangement. An agreement as to payment—"

"All three of you cross or none at all," Charon booms inside my head, the sound echoing as if we're in a cave, although his voice to my ears is soft. "Come to Chiswick Mall at midnight and bring two coins for the ferryman."

And with that he turns and leaves, returning to his buddies.

Sarroch follows him with his eyes, looking incredibly unhappy. But there's not much he can do. We have to sort out this hungry ghost problem, so I guess that means all three of us are crossing.

20

We settle ourselves down in a nearby pub to wait until midnight. It's one of those cosy ones, with dark wood panelling on the walls and old prints of sailing boats. Appetising smells waft out from the kitchen as the door swings open and shut to let the waitresses through as they carry or clear dishes. When a waitress walks past our table carrying one plate heaped with bangers and mash, and the other with fish and chips, my stomach rumbles and my mouth waters.

We order food and drinks – I'm particularly delighted to discover they have some wonderful craft ales. Nothing beats a good British ale in my book. Especially when it comes from a small, independent brewer. Something about knowing the care and love that went into producing the ale.

I sigh with satisfaction after the first sip of my pint, and again after the second. Crisp and citrusy, with a slight, bitter tang on the finish. Delish. "Did anyone else notice that Charon completely changed his tune about taking Sarroch across when he caught sight of me?" I ask. "Or am I being self-obsessed?"

"I did," Sarroch replies. His expression makes it clear just how unhappy he is with that state of things.

"Yeah, he seemed quite taken with you," Pree says. "Why is that?"

"I have no idea. I'd love to think it was my looks, but somehow I doubt I'm his type."

"Whatever it is, I don't like it," Sarroch says.

"I don't like it either," I say aloud. "But I don't see that we have a choice. And anyway, it's better that you don't go alone. What if you're unable to lay to rest what needs to be laid to rest, because your hungry ghost takes over?"

"What is this hungry ghost?" Pree asks.

I quickly bring her up to date about Sarroch. Since it seems that she is now stuck with coming with us to the underworld, there's really no point in keeping anything from her. I gloss over how close I came to being destroyed, because from the way Sarroch's features crumple, this is really hard for him to hear. I don't minimise just how powerful he is, though, nor how dangerous he can be if he isn't in control. I want Pree armed with all the facts to give her the best possible opportunity to take care of herself if things go south.

Which they hopefully won't. As I talk, I reach up with my magic, towards the skies where Qinglong rests. I can still feel her, although that's not precise enough a word. I feel her in the same way that a louse feels a tiny patch of skin on an elephant, without ever being able to take in the *whole* elephant. She's there, but that's all I'm able to process.

Pree listens to me, her face serious but utterly bland. I was expecting some shock, maybe a wary glance towards Sarroch.

Nothing.

"Doesn't this freak you out at least just a little bit?" I ask her.

She shrugs. "Freaking out about it wouldn't change anything, would it? If anything, I find it interesting. And it's not such a great surprise. After all, we've got so many stories about monsters—they have to originate from somewhere." Sarroch winces at the word 'monster'. Pree doesn't notice.

"But you're not scared?" I ask. "Self-preservation isn't screaming at you not to come with us to the underworld?" If it is, maybe there's a way to convince Charon to only take Sarroch and me. He didn't seem that fussed about Pree.

"You know me. I live by the motto that if there's something I'm afraid of, I go charging at it until I get past it and stop being scared."

"Yeah, that's a very good life philosophy in normal circumstances, not so much when it comes to the supernatural. When those little hairs are standing on edge at the back of your neck and you get that horrible skin-crawling feeling, that is a very clear signal to get the hell out—not to charge in."

"Potato, potah-to." From Pree's expression, she clearly thinks she's agreeing with me when it's obvious she doesn't get it.

"No. It's like... For example, didn't you feel anything earlier, during the confrontation between Sarroch and Charon?"

Our food arrives, interrupting us. Oh, sweet gravy. The Brits get a bad rep for their food. Given the culinary delights Southeast Asia is able to muster in even the most humble of street stalls, it's clear good old Blighty can't compete.

But when it comes to gravy... I would go out on a limb and say that no other country in the world possesses our skill at producing gravy. The deep plate in front of me is drowning in a dark, glistening gravy of caramelised onion, out of which is protruding an island of colcannon mash, topped with three plump sage and pork sausages.

Heaven, heaven, heaven on a plate.

I tuck into my first sausage, savouring the slightly burnt flavour of the gravy against the creaminess of the mash and rich, herbiness of the sausage, while next to me wholesale slaughter begins.

No, Sarroch has not suddenly taken leave of his manners and started to eat like an animal—that's just Pree.

She's always eaten like a starving woman receiving her first meal in weeks. That girl eats like a horse, drinks like a fish, and somehow remains just about on the right side of lean. She has the most crazy metabolism, and if she doesn't hoover up food like it's going out of fashion, she gets unhealthily skinny.

"Magic help me," Sarroch mutters. "I don't think even werewolves eat so ravenously."

"There's no point trying to talk to her while she's eating," I reply. "It's like she disappears when the food arrives. She'll inhale her food in a few minutes, and then she'll be able to speak again."

Sarroch and I continue eating at a normal pace, and we're not even close to halfway done when, true to form, Pree finishes. She turns to me with a happy smile.

"Fan-*ta*-bulous. And to answer your earlier question, I didn't feel anything between Sarroch and Charon."

I frown. "That's really weird."

Normally, although Mundanes can't sense magic in the true sense of the word, they have enough primal awareness to grow uncomfortable when there's too much magic in the air, or when they find themselves face to face with a dangerous predator. Some kind of recognition deeply buried in their lizard brains awakens, making them suddenly decide they don't want to be here.

Pree, however, seems to be lacking that. And then there's also the fact that Sarroch's compelling didn't work on her before.

"I have to admit I have very little idea about what is normal for Mundanes and what isn't," Sarroch says. "But suffice to say that normally I can control a Mundane in my sleep. The fact that I couldn't earlier is...interesting."

I reach for Pree with my magic again, but she just feels like a completely normal human. Not even one Touched by magic.

Sarroch frowns. "It will mean, Pree, that you'll need to be all the more sharp and do exactly as Apiya and I tell you. If you don't have any warning centres of your own to let you know when danger is coming—"

"You will let me know and I'll do exactly what you say," Pree finishes with a smile. "No problemo."

I really hope she means it.

21

By the time midnight rolls around, I've drifted off with my head against Sarroch's shoulder in a haze of jetlag and bangers and mash food coma, underscored by the lovely warm buzz brought about by the ale. I'm not drunk, just tired.

I wake up abruptly when a hand shakes me gently.

"Time to go, Apiya," Sarroch says.

I rub two hands over my face and shake myself quickly to wake up. "Okay. Okay. I'm ready." My body disagrees. It feels sluggish and heavy and slow. It groans at me, yearning for bed.

I stand up and move about a bit to help the pins and needles dissipate—I was sleeping in an awkward position that cut off circulation to a lot of my left side. Around us the pub staff are closing down for the night—we're the last ones to leave.

Finally, feeling a tad more alert, I glance over at Pree and Sarroch. They're both looking at me. They seem smug.

"What have you two been talking about?" I ask suspiciously.

"Oh, the usual," Pree replies innocently. "Sarroch now knows all of your dirty stories from when we were young, of course."

From the grin on Sarroch's face, he might not know all of them, but it's clear Pree told him quite a bit. With friends like that, who needs enemies, eh?

"I won't expect you to try to jump across puddles to impress me," Sarroch tells me in a low voice as we make our way out of the pub. I glare at both him and Pree. That will be referring to the unbelievably embarrassing time I tried to impress a crush at school by jumping over a puddle, missed, and face planted into it. I'm not sure what's more embarrassing, really—that I fell, or that I thought jumping a puddle would impress a boy.

To be fair to Pree, although she laughed like a hyena at the time, she also swapped half her clothes with me so I wouldn't just be wearing soaking, muddy clothing all day at school.

"And to think he never asked you out after that," Pree jokes as we step outside.

We're back on the pedestrian waterfront walkway. The air is cooler now that night is deeply settled. The smell of brackish water rises up from the river. This part of the Thames is still tidal, and the tide is currently low, revealing wide, silt-and-algae-covered pebbles. A few forlorn items are scattered about—a single shoe, a torn glove, a couple of crushed coke cans. Beyond the naked shore, the river gleams, the water placid, reflecting the moon overhead.

We walk down the waterfront until we reach the spot Charon indicated on Chiswick Mall. Part of me seriously can't believe that this is where he chooses to operate.

You could not get a more middle-class—nay bourgeois

—area if you tried. At least in Panong, the Mayak go for areas that are a bit rundown, a bit alternative. Here it seems the supernatural are quite comfortable in areas that could serve as a setting to the British version of the Stepford Wives. Manicured hedges, Edwardian houses with large bay windows, and, of course, expensive cars parked in the street out front.

Although I suppose the key difference is that fancy areas of London tend to have old buildings—the very kind of buildings that are so necessary to the Mayak.

A brick wall separates the waterfront walkway from the Thames's edge, topped by a steel railing. We climb over the wall and railing, dropping down on the slippery pebbles below. The impact isn't that much, but I feel a dull throb of pain from the injury in my leg, the one from when I crashed my motorbike.

Charon is waiting for us right by the water's edge. A long, narrow, and shallow boat—a punt, the kind that is famously punted down the river Cam, in Cambridge—has been dragged up onto the pebbles.

The shadows are thicker around the ferryman than they are anywhere else. I can't see much more than his outline, when I can see everything else around him perfectly well, courtesy of the virtually full moon.

A reminder that our deadline is virtually upon us. Tomorrow night, if we haven't got a mating bond in place, my deal with the Mayak Elders will be forfeit.

The one thing I can see clearly about Charon is his pale green eye as it glows with restrained power, like coals that have been left to smoulder overnight but are ready to erupt into flame the moment the right material is presented to them.

"Two coins for the ferryman." Charon's voice is so deep, I swear I can hear it from my feet. And it once again has an echo it shouldn't possess given that we're out in the open.

He puts his palm out. Somehow his hand pierces through the shadows that cloak him. It looks like a perfectly normal human hand—thick-jointed and blunt-nailed. The kind of hand that would be used to punt boats across rivers.

"I pay for my passage," Sarroch says in a formal tone, handing him what looks like two fifty pence coins.

I'm about to question whether such a trip costs more than a quid, but as soon as the coins drop into Charon's hands, they turn large and thick and gold. I only get a quick glimpse of them before Charon's fist closes around them, drawing them back into the shadows.

The hand extends towards me next. "Two coins for the ferryman."

I fish some coins out of my pocket. One twenty pence, and one pound.

"I pay for my passage," I say, matching Sarroch's tone.

In Charon's hands, the coins transform once again. This time I see them a little better. Symbols unlike anything we have in Panong—including in the Mayak spaces there—are engraved along the edge. In the centre, a snake swallows its tail. The Ourobos.

Once again, the hand disappears back into the shadow and this time returns for Pree. She looks at me. "Since the coins transform anyway, you reckon I can just give him two pennies?"

Before I can answer, she drops the two small copper coins into the waiting hand. They transform without any trouble and she smiles, delighted.

Charon steps back and gestures towards the boat.

Sarroch climbs on first, then me, and finally Pree. As I pass Charon, I swear I can feel his green eye burning a hole in my back.

He climbs in when we are all settled. If this was a Mundane boat, it would have needed to be pushed out into the water before Charon could climb on, but this is not a Mundane boat.

A long pole appears in Charon's hands, and as he pushes it against the shore, we are suddenly in deep waters. Mist curls along the surface ahead.

I turn back to look at the shore. It already seems far away and somehow indistinct. Mist starts to gather there as well, and soon the mist grows so thick that I can't see the shore at all.

It's slightly creepy and unsettling, but as I look back, I also catch sight of Pree behind me. She's wearing the kind of excited grin normally seen on young children about to start a rollercoaster.

Suddenly her attitude angers me, and I grab her wrist. "This is serious, Pree," I whisper, hopefully low enough for Charon not to hear. "It's not a game. It's not a ride. You don't mess around with this. Okay?" I only just manage to stop myself from giving her a little shake.

Of all of us, she is by far the most defenceless, and yet nothing I say seems to be able to draw that fact into her skull. I'm afraid for her. I'm also afraid that she'll do something reckless and endanger us all.

I really, really couldn't bear it if she got hurt tonight because of me.

"I know," she tells me soothingly, rubbing her hand on my arm. "Don't worry. It'll be fine."

At the front of the boat, Sarroch is peering at the darkness, but since I'm behind him, I can't make out his facial expression. The tension in his shoulders, though, is obvious.

I wonder what we will find when we reach the underworld. I suddenly wish I shared Pree's confidence that all will work out.

———

THE CROSSING TAKES A LONG TIME. A LONG TIME DURING which we don't see or hear a single thing, save for the whispering of the water against our boat and the wet sounds as Charon plunges his pole into the river.

The mist has become so thick it's hard to even know whether we're moving forward. It's like we're suspended in a world of grey. The water is perfectly black, and there are no reassuring moon or stars overhead, just uninterrupted darkness.

Pree has finally taken measure of the seriousness of the hour, and she's silent and sombre. Which is a relief.

Finally, the mist parts ahead of us. If I didn't have magic, I'd have thought we had gotten turned around and returned to the edge of the Thames.

Beyond the edge of the water, all that is visible are large, round pebbles, slick with silt and algae. In short, exactly the kind of shore we have just left, save for the fact that beyond the shore, the mist is still too thick for us to see past.

But despite appearances, we are far from the Mundane world. I don't have to reach out with my magic to sense it. The air is thick with magic, but it's not the buzzing feeling against my skin kind. Rather, it's something that feels more damp, like cold, thick and soupy air before a storm.

Sometime during the crossing, Charon's boat changed. The flat, low nose has lengthened and curved up, and it now holds a single light that glows a sickly green. The boat itself is still long and narrow, but the edges now curve up, where before they were straight.

Charon himself also looks different. He still has his flat cap, but now it looks a bit more like a sailor's cap. The peak of the cap keeps his face shrouded in shadows, but his green eye still burns. His hair and beard are long, trailing down his back and chest. Whether he still has his plumber's crack is anybody's guess, because his jumper has turned into a tattered and ripped but long robe-like garment that hangs in ragged ribbons about his knees.

He somehow gives both the impression of skeletal thinness and the kind of brawny strength it would take to punt along a boat with three people in it.

He pushes the little boat right up to the pebbled shore, the hull shivering and groaning as it scrapes against the stones.

"Welcome to the underworld." His voice booms, filling the air all around us as powerfully as an opera singer fills an auditorium. "You may seek the one you came to see."

We climb out of the boat one by one and stand on the muddy, slippery shore. I'm relieved to see that Pree's serious and tense demeanour remains rather than her looking around her in wonder. She's not treating this as some kind of joke or fun ride, which makes me feel a lot better about her safety.

"What now?" she asks.

Sarroch takes a deep, shuddering breath. His hands are shaking. "Now I call Eyva to me, I suppose." His voice is thick with emotion.

I can imagine the thoughts that must be running through his head. Will she remember him? Will she look as he remembers her, or will she be some ghoulish apparition?

"Will it help if we focus on her as well?" I ask.

Sarroch nods.

"I've never seen her," Pree points out.

"It doesn't matter," Sarroch replies. "It's not about picturing what she looks like, it's about calling who she is. You know a bit about her, so just focus on that."

"I'll keep my hand on you," I tell Sarroch as I come to stand next to him, placing my hand on his arm. My hand with the silver beneath the skin. "In case anything happens."

"Yes. Good idea." His lips are pressed into a line, his eyes are grim.

We all fall silent as we focus on Eyva. I reach out with my magic as well, and after a moment, it feels as if I can almost sense the edges of something. I'm not sure if it's my imagination or if I can truly make out little scraps of... something, beyond the mist. I wouldn't know how to begin to quantify it—I can't even tell if what I'm sensing is something alive in the true sense of the world or just an energy like what I get from a chair or a rock.

Still, I feel encouraged, and I double down and focus harder. I glance over at Sarroch to see if he's also getting something, and I gasp. It's hard to make out in as much detail as in Pragya's mirror, but I can definitely see the hungry ghost wrapped around him.

"What?" he asks urgently. "Can you see her?"

"Not her but your ghost. It's to your right."

He turns his head and squints down. I feel a brief buzzing feeling against my skin as his magic wells up into the air, and then it abruptly dissipates. "I can just about feel it," he says.

"I can't see anything," Pree says. "Oh, wait. Now I can. Is

that the hungry ghost?" She's pointing ahead of us. "Wow, that's...that's *cool*."

Before us, the mist gathers, slowly swirling itself into a shape. A humanlike shape.

I feel Sarroch's muscles tense up beneath my hand. "That's not my hungry ghost. That's Eyva."

22

I t takes time for Eyva to coalesce in front of us. At first she's little more than a faint, blurry outline. But even as she takes more solid form, she remains indistinct. She has no face, no clothes. Just a general shape.

Behind her, the flickers continue to wink in and out of the mist. I'm no clearer on what they are, but they seem separate from Eyva.

"Are you guys also seeing the stuff in the mist?"

"What stuff?" Pree asks.

Sarroch shakes his head once, eyes riveted on Eyva's shape.

"Never mind," I reply.

My magic works differently to Sarroch's, and this is the world of spirits, after all, so I'm bound to perceive things differently from him. I don't want to be distracted or distract him from what we came here for, though. The intricacies of how my magic works in the underworld is a question for another time.

The shape continues to thicken before us, Eyva growing more and more real.

Sarroch has paled to the point that he's going grey. "I don't know if I can do this." His voice is choked, his eyes wide.

"I've got you," I remind him, gripping his arm harder with my left hand. "You can do this. You need to do this."

He swallows and nods. His breathing is heavy.

After a while, the shape stops becoming more detailed.

"You took from me," a female voice says mournfully. As with Charon's voice, it rings out all around us, but while I start at the noise, Pree doesn't react.

"Did you hear that?" I ask her.

She raises an eyebrow in question and shakes her head.

"I'm sorry," Sarroch whispers.

"I have been incomplete all this time," Eyva continues, her voice hauntingly sad.

Sarroch looks as if he has just been hit. Hard. And suddenly his hungry ghost takes on a more solid appearance. Its distended belly a fat, bloated drop, its mouth still buried in the side of Sarroch's neck. Its arms and legs seem to have thickened, wrapped tightly around him.

"Magic help me, Eyva, I never meant for that... If I'd had any idea... Have you been in pain? Have you...suffered?"

"The dead don't suffer. But I have been incomplete."

"I will give back what I...I will give back what I held onto. I'm sorry, Eyva. I'm so sorry."

Suddenly I have an idea. I reach for Sarroch's hungry ghost with my magic. Maybe there's something I can do to nudge things along, or ease things somehow.

I only just manage to repress a cry of disgust. Connecting to it is like sticking my hand in a bucket full of cold, wriggling worms.

The sensation crawls all over my skin, but still I maintain the connection. If Sarroch held on to something of

Eyva's, it must be the same thing that is feeding the hungry ghost, so logic dictates that if I follow my sense of the hungry ghost, I should reach the thing keeping it tied to Sarroch.

Before I can do that, though, the cold, crawling sensation suddenly flares up along the back of my head as if something has just approached me from behind. I cry out in fright and spin around.

As I do, I let go of Sarroch. There is no one behind me.

"Will you show yourself to me?" Sarroch asks. "Show yourself fully? You don't know how many times I've wished for that."

I scan the river shore behind me quickly, but it's definitely empty save for Charon and his boat. And yet the sensation at the back of my head...

I turn back.

The mist that is Eyva swirls. "No. I am not cruel. The past is for the dead. The living must look to the future."

The goosebumps on my skin warn me that something subtle is shifting. I check on Sarroch, but his eyes are still normal.

"It wouldn't be cruel." Sarroch's tone has changed. There's much less emotion to it. "I want to see you."

Eyva remains silent.

"You know what, this is a waste of time. We are leaving. Apiya," he snaps.

Sarroch went to all weirdly cold and distant when we went to Pragya's hut, and the hungry ghost likely influenced him to get him away from a situation that could be a threat to it. The change of mood right now is weird, so I don't let it continue.

I place my left hand on Sarroch's arm once more, pushing my silver to the surface.

He lets out a very feline yell of pain, wrenching himself away from me. For a fraction of a second, his eyes are filled with a powerful burning anger.

I keep my left hand out at the ready. The anger in his eyes burns away almost as quickly as it flared up.

"Did the hungry ghost get a hold of you?" I ask him cautiously.

He blinks a couple of times, looking confused. "I don't know. I suddenly felt so angry—I'm not even sure why. It was...like it was hard to control myself."

I nod. "Yeah, something about you felt wrong."

"Yes, it did to me, too. Foreign."

"Must have been the ghost."

"It must have been. I hate this, Apiya. I really hate this."

"We just have to keep going and it will be over. I think I might be able to help, by the way. By connecting to your hungry ghost. Help nudge things along, maybe, or help you release whatever you have to release."

Sarroch nods. "That's a good idea. This doesn't feel like it's going to be easy."

"Agreed."

Sarroch takes my hand and his eyes connect with mine. "Thank you. For being here. I don't think I'd have been able to do this on my own."

"You don't have to thank me. Let's stay focused on the task at hand. Once it's all done, I'll be as smug and 'told you that you needed my help' as you like."

"What about me, what can I do?" Pree asks.

"Stand behind me. Keep a hand on my shoulder so I can feel you there, and keep an eye out for anything approaching us from behind. I got the feeling of something coming for me from behind, and that pulled me out of what

I was doing. It was probably just a trick from the ghost, but if I know you've got my back, that will help."

Pree shifts positions to be a little behind me. She's resting the tip of her cricket bat on the ground, leaning her hand on the handle.

If there truly is something coming from behind, she might not be able to see anything. But I'm feeling pretty confident that was the hungry ghost messing with me, so if she can help me stay anchored, that should help me fight against the horrible, crawling sensation.

Taking a breath, I reach for the hungry ghost once more.

"Stop that," Sarroch snaps at me.

I tap a silvered finger against his shoulder. It makes a hissing sound, and he winces.

"Your hungry ghost seems a lot stronger out here," I tell him.

"Agreed." His tone is back to normal. "Which makes sense, since we are in the underworld, which must be a good environment for it. And then it has me, and possibly even Eyva's spirit, to draw from."

I grimace. The last time the hungry ghost was in a strong position, in the werecat realm, it came very close to destroying me. Not much we can do about it, though. We just have to get going and hope we can take care of it. "Okay, let's try again."

Sarroch nods at me and turns back to face the ghost of his dead mate.

I take a deep breath and plunge my awareness back into the hungry ghost. This time the awful cold, wriggling feeling erupts all over my body, as if I've been dunked face down into a full-body-sized container of maggots.

It's all I can do not to gag. Pree is a reassuringly solid

presence at my shoulder, and I'm really glad I asked her to hold on to me.

I push on, following what I can feel of the hungry ghost. The deeper I go, the more I can sense Sarroch beyond it. It's like I pushed my awareness inside of Sarroch via the ghost. I can sense him trying to let go, but whatever it is he's trying to release, I can tell that it's stuck tight.

The wriggling sensation gets worse, and then suddenly I can feel it inside my mouth and throat, inside my nose and ears, against my eyes. I make a strangled noise.

"Api? You okay?" Pree asks.

"Just... Don't let go of me." I'm almost surprised that I'm able to speak when my mouth feels like it's been filled with maggots.

It's hard to focus, but I do my best, reminding myself that there are no maggots. It's just the hungry ghost messing with my perception centres.

My perception centres. That gives me an idea. If they're part of me, then ultimately I'm the one who controls them. I reach out for the wriggling sensation all over my body and push it away. I can't make it disappear, but I can make it feel faint, like I've just taken a dive underwater, so I'm only faintly aware of what's going on at the surface.

Better. Much, much better. The wriggling is no longer overwhelming, leaving me free to focus my magic where I want.

It doesn't take me much time to find the thing that keeps the ghost tethered to Sarroch.

It feels like a lump. I get the sense that it's old, so old that it has gradually fused with its surroundings, becoming as much a part of Sarroch as his arms and legs.

I'm not sure what that lump is supposed to represent, but it feels like it once was of vibrant colours, whereas now it's a dark, murky colour that matches the underworld. Like rot and death. The lump is twisted and misshapen, and the energy of the hungry ghost pulses greedily around it, greasy and thick as oil.

Before I can sense anything more about it, a painful impact sends me reeling to the side. I don't have time to regain my balance or process what's happening before two hands close around my throat.

23

S arroch's eyes are blank and dead. The hungry ghost seems to be everywhere, not just hanging from his side, but wrapped around him like a cocoon. There is a powerful stench in the air, like rotten vinegar.

I don't hear the word with my ears, but I sense it.

Mine.

My hands scrabble at Sarroch's, trying to wrench them off my throat, which feels like it's on fire. My mouth is open, instinctively trying to suck in air. The pressure in my head is painful, black splotches appearing in my vision.

I try to wheeze Sarroch's name to call him back to himself, but I can't make a sound.

Something crashes into the side of his head with a meaty *thwack,* and he releases me, staggering a little. I draw a deep, shuddering breath, and only then realise that in my panic I completely forgot to use my silver hand.

Pree lifts her cricket bat and hits Sarroch again. It cracks heavily against his shoulder. In a human, that would have been enough to break bone. But this is Sarroch, and instead the shock of it seems to return his eyes to normal.

"Apiya," he gasps. "What... Magic help me, are you hurt?" His breathing is ragged, as if he has just run a great distance. He reaches for me, his eyes scanning my throat. His face crumples, and I'm guessing he spotted a bit of bruising.

"I'm fine."

He shakes his head. "You're not. We're stopping right now. I'm not putting you in any more danger. I can't bear being made to attack you again, Apiya. This is...This is too wrong for words. We're leaving right now, and I'll just have to find some other way to fix this."

"No. We're staying and seeing this through."

"Apiya, I can't bear this. It's turning me into the monster I've spent my whole life trying to prove I'm not. I don't want to hurt you."

"It's not turning you into anything. You're still you. And you'll hurt me far more if we leave. What if your hungry ghost keeps growing stronger? What if one day it takes over when you're in Panong? What if the hungry ghost makes you destroy everything when you're in my house, with Chai and Hunter and all my animals there? With the pari-pari youngling there?" The very thought makes my throat grow tight.

Sarroch closes his eyes, looking sickened. "I'll have to exile myself—"

"Where? Where can you go that this kind of destruction wouldn't be a problem? We *have* to see this through. We might have given the ghost more strength by coming here, and how do we know that it won't be able to use it in the Mundane world? The risk to me right now is acceptable if it means we sort this out. You have too much power for you to allow anything else to control it."

Sarroch looks at me, eyes wide and haunted. "Apiya, what if I really hurt you doing this? What if I kill you?"

"You won't kill me. I'm resilient."

"And I'll be hammering you with my bat the moment you try anything dodgy," Pree tells him. "I might not be able to see magical stuff, but I sure as shit saw you try to strangle Api." She lifts her bat and pats it. "I told you this is useful."

"It is," Sarroch agrees. "Thank you for not hesitating to strike me."

"No worries. Tell you what. I'll keep an eye on you and crack you about the head the moment you look like you might hurt Api. No hard feelings if I get it wrong and hit you for no reason, though."

"No hard feelings *at all*," Sarroch replies with feeling. "I'd rather you did that than the alternative."

I shoot Pree a grateful look. "I don't know if some sort of fate intervened to bring us together at the airport, but I'm really glad you're here."

She smiles. "Me too."

I turn back to Sarroch. "So there you go. We have a plan for keeping me safe. And next time I won't forget to use my silver hand. Why do you think the hungry ghost had you try to strangle me rather than use your magic like last time, by the way?"

"I'm not sure. I think it has something to with the fact that there's no metal down here. To do what I did at the werecat realm, it helps for there to be larger bits of metal for me to gain momentum with before I start...tearing everything apart. I could still do it to the both of you, but it would take me a moment to get focused—plenty of time for you and Pree to intervene. When I...um." Sarroch briefly looks he might be sick at having to say that he tried to strangle me.

"What the hungry ghost made me do was possibly a quicker way to get you to stop."

I nod. "Okay, well, that's an important thing to know. It means the hungry ghost understands how your magic works and is able to strategise. It almost sounds like it's conscious."

"I suppose it must be, after a fashion, since it's feeding off my consciousness."

I look at the ugly grey creature wrapped around Sarroch. "Well, at least I'm glad that you're not able to use your magic quite like at the werecat's realm. As much as being strangled is not high on my list of things to experience, it's definitely still better than what happened back then."

"And there's always my cricket bat." Pree grins and taps it against the ground. "I was actually decent at cricket at school. Never thought it would come in useful."

I realise that I was wrong earlier when I got angry at her for not being serious enough. It wouldn't achieve anything if she was worried or scared right now, and if anything her cheerful mood helps to relax the situation a little.

"Let me rest," Eyva's spirit whispers. "Please let me be complete and let me rest."

Sarroch looks haunted at the words. Haunted and devoured by guilt.

I touch a hand to his shoulder. "You didn't know, and you certainly can't be blamed for something you didn't even realise was happening."

He grimaces. "Easier said than done."

"Also, if the ghost is lashing out, it must be because it's feeling threatened," Pree points out.

"That's very true," I reply. "It lashed out in a similar way at the werecat realm when Pragya wanted to cut it away. That must mean we're getting close. Let's try again."

We get into position, Pree lifting her cricket bat and focusing on Sarroch's face. I hold her shoulder with one hand for reassurance, Sarroch's with the other ready to burn him with silver.

We make an odd triangle, the three of us.

"Okay, here goes." I take a deep breath, centre myself, and plunge forward again.

24

This time, because I'm expecting it, the horrid crawling sensation is less of a shock, even though it erupts all over my skin at once. I squeeze Sarroch and Pree's shoulders. The reassurance that they are both there, solid and real—alive—does a lot to help with the nauseating sensations.

Same as last time, I find a way to push the wriggling back enough that it's no longer overwhelming, leaving me to go searching for that lump again. I find it quickly this time. It's every bit as twisted, ugly, dark, and rotten as before.

This time, though, I also pick up a powerful resistance wrapped around it, a resistance that's directly working against Sarroch's attempts at letting go. Woven through that resistance is the slow throb of the greedy ghost's energy.

I reach for the lump and try to shove at it, hoping to get something moving or dislodged so that Sarroch can then release whatever it is he needs to release to make that lump disappear.

As I do, it's like my sense of Sarroch sort of slips aside, replaced by wriggling, ice cold rage. Like the container of worms I've been lowered into suddenly turns conscious and all of those worms turn to attack me.

I don't even stop to think, sending the silver shooting forward in my left hand. I manage to do that without breaking connection. The focus required means I can't really pay attention to anything else, although I do feel the ripple of an impact jarring up my left arm.

That must have been Pree and her bat.

"I'm back, I'm back," Sarroch rasps. "Thank you, Priscilla."

The sensation of him attempting to release the lump returns, and again it begins to throb dully, like a noxious resentment at this attack against it.

I don't try to shove the lump again, but instead, I pause to observe it a little while longer. I can sense the hungry ghost around part of me as well now, probably because of my extended connection with the lump. The ghost feels cold and full of that awful rotten vinegary smell. It's greedy, angry, but I can also sense fear beneath it all.

That's good. That means I'm definitely a threat to it. I reach towards the lump but instead of trying to dislodge it, this time I try to connect to it directly.

The reaction is so rapid and so intense, it feels like I touched my fingers to an electric plug socket. A wave of impressions jolts through me, so powerful that at first all I'm aware of is pain so huge it overwhelms everything. I break the connection with the lump.

"Are you okay?" Pree asks me.

"Yeah." I'm not entirely sure that's true. My head is spinning, and everything in my body tingles with a weird kind of buzzing aftershock. Both my voice and my legs feel shaky.

Once I have taken a couple of breaths, I dive in again. This time I'm able to get more of a sense of what the lump is throwing at me. Pain and grief, mixed with a rage so thick and black, it burns like molten lava. And beneath it all, a yawning chasm of shame.

The impressions keep flying at me. Pain and destruction that feel foreign to Sarroch. It's not until I get a visual impression, faster than a blink, that I realise it belongs to the people and animals Sarroch slaughtered.

He didn't just destroy a civilisation. He laid waste to everything in that part of the world. Trees, plants, animals. Rocks reduced to sand. Scorched earth isn't quite enough to encapsulate the thoroughness of the destruction he brought about. There was nothing left after he was done. Not even insects in the ground.

The pain and shame wrapped up in that are so strong that even though they're not mine, it's so crushing I have a hard time breathing through the sensation of it.

More and more impressions fly at me, coming thick and fast. Sarroch's attempts at finding any survivors from the civilisation he destroyed, in order to try to somehow make amends. Having failed, I see him building, by hand and without using magic, monuments to commemorate the people he extinguished. There are many, but I only recognise one as still standing today, and it's obviously since been taken over by a Mundane religion: Angkor Wat, in Cambodia.

I see him slowly healing the soil he destroyed, then replanting trees and reintroducing animals to the area. I see his attempts at helping other humans beyond the carnage zone, both the ones with magic and without. And all the while carrying this crushing shame, both at what he'd done and at his failure to keep Eyva safe.

I hear the swirl of stories about him, both from Mayak and humans, depicting him as the kind of evil monster that stalks through old folk tales. Each one of those stories carries with it a razor-sharp pain that makes me wince even though I only get a faint echo of it.

The swirl of stories builds and builds over the centuries, dogging him, until one day Sarroch gives up, locking the whole thing away—the guilt, the shame, the rage, the pain. He stops his attempts at making amends, instead becoming closed off and aloof.

What must it be like to have carried all this for centuries? And all of it drip-feeding the hungry ghost, not only keeping it alive, but gradually increasing its strength.

It might not excuse what he did, but a lifetime of loneliness and shame that stretches over centuries, not to mention centuries of carrying all that foul black stuff inside him, is more than punishment enough.

I reach for the dark lump and do the only thing I can think of doing. I send it love and forgiveness.

I have no idea whether or not I love Sarroch. *Way* too early for all of that business. But I do know that it's time that he found a little peace. If anything, it will have been the lack of forgiveness that keeps the twisted blackened lump inside him. And what has that achieved?

Nothing more than feeding the parasitic hungry ghost that almost tried to bring about the same kind of destruction all over again.

I pour all the love and forgiveness I can into the blackened lump, and Hunter suddenly appears in my mind's eye. I don't know that I'm particularly good at forgiveness—I'm not a saint, far from it. But I've had a few years at the hands of a true master of forgiveness.

Hunter loves and forgives me even when I genuinely am a shitty human. Which has happened on *numerous* occasions, and yet he has never wavered, even when my shitti-ness relates to me being a less than stellar dog owner.

As soon as this thought occurs to me, I'm able to find a sort of cache within myself, containing all the unwavering, unfailing, and unconditional love Hunter has given me over the years.

I direct all of it to Sarroch's twisted, horrid lump.

Sarroch gasps, his eyes going wide. The wriggling sensa-tion on my skin worsens, the rotten, vinegary smell growing more powerful until I could almost choke on it.

And then something shifts. I don't know what Sarroch does, exactly, but something clicks or maybe something breaks. Suddenly the twisted black lump erupts into a rainbow of colours, and then it, the hungry ghost, and Eyva's mist-form are all drawn together, twisting around each other.

"What is that?" Pree asks.

"That is Eyva." Sarroch's voice is thick with tears, but although his eyes are shiny, they remain dry.

The twisting subsides until before us are a woman and a tigress. The woman is small and her colouring is deeply faded, almost grey, but I can make out enough to know that she had the same kind of colouring as Pragya. Her hair is long and black, and her face looks like in life it would have been very expressive. She is not pretty, not in the traditional sense of the word, but there is something charismatic and striking about her. A generous mouth and a slightly upturned nose. Almond-shaped eyes that are quite wide apart. Her tigress is small, with stripes closer together than the other tigers I've seen so far. She also has a kind of mane, or maybe it's a ruff.

Both of them are barely material enough to be visible. Eyva smiles at Sarroch, while he devours her with his eyes.

For a moment, it seems like the world has disappeared, like Pree and I do not exist.

I keep totally silent, and Pree does the same.

Eyva speaks a few words to Sarroch that I don't understand. He replies in the same language, followed by a low rumble that sounds like it comes from his tiger.

Eyva smiles wider. She turns to look at me and says a few words.

Then she and her tigress turn and walk off into the mist, fading away and melding with it.

For a moment, no one moves. And then Sarroch collapses slowly, bonelessly, to his knees.

25

I give Sarroch a few moments before I come sit next to him.

After a while, I nudge him with my shoulder. "You okay?"

He exhales a deep, ragged sigh. "I still miss her. I always will. She was everything to me. And it still kills me that I wasn't able to keep her safe. Even though I've had centuries to get used to it, it still hurts that she died." He turns to me. "But you can't imagine the relief. I feel like I've been going through life with a boulder on my back, and today I put it down. And she looked at peace, before she disappeared. She told me so as well, and I think she told the truth." He glances at me. "You said you saw something before. Can you get a sense of what the underworld is like for the dead?"

I keep my eyes from the mist. The shimmers I see there make me uncomfortable, and to be honest, now that we're done, I just want to get out of here.

"Not really. And I don't really want to try. I think there are things we're not supposed to know."

"You're right." Sarroch smiles at me. "The other thing

Eyva told me was to get back to the world of the living and enjoy my life. I think I should follow her advice."

Sarroch pushes himself to standing and reaches a hand down, pulling me up to my feet.

"That sounds like a good plan," I tell him. "Especially if this plan includes a hot shower and a comfy bed."

"That can be arranged."

We turn back to where Pree is waiting for us. I reach her side. "Are you okay?"

"Fine. I didn't really do much other than occasionally use my cricket bat. That was wild, though."

"Yeah, it was, but I'm glad it's all done. Let's get back to the boat."

We all head back to where Charon has been waiting. He's still at the back of the boat as he was before. The front of it still arcs up, curving back down at the top to dangle that single, sickly green lantern.

I glance back over my shoulder at the place where Eyva disappeared. I can see more and more flickers, light, and a sense of something, or maybe even people, beyond the mist. I shiver—my unease deepening. I'll be feeling much happier when I'm back on the other side, back at the dirty edge of the River Thames rather than at the strange edge of the river Styx.

Pree climbs into the boat first. Sarroch climbs in after her and turns back, holding out his hand to help me up.

Smiling at the chivalrous gesture, I reach for his hand and for the boat's edge.

Both my hands slip off, failing to make contact. I snort with annoyance at my clumsiness and reach again. And again I slip. It's weird, like Sarroch's hand and the boat are both made of glass or something equally slippery.

"What's going on?" Sarroch frowns.

He reaches down to grab me, but fails to get my wrist, just missing me.

My initial annoyance is rapidly turning to panic as I scramble at the boat. I can still see the grain of the wood it's made of, but every time I touch it, I slide right off. Sarroch is leaning so far out of the boat now that he's in danger of falling out, but no matter what he does, he can't seem to grab me.

It's as if the boat, Sarroch, and I have become magnets with matching poles, repelling each other.

Sarroch tries to climb out of the boat and fails.

"Charon," Sarroch growls, "Stop whatever it is you're doing and let Apiya back onto the boat."

"Only the living may leave the underworld," Charon booms.

He touches his pole to the water and all of a sudden, the boat is no longer at the edge but way out into the river.

Horror unlike anything I've ever experienced roils in my belly.

This cannot be.

Sarroch is roaring for Charon to stop, scrambling at the edge of the boat, desperately trying to climb out of it, but he is repelled by it as much as I was, unable to throw himself into the water and towards the shore.

Pree is also yelling, and she launches herself at Charon with her bat, attempting to stop him from punting away. Her bat connects soundlessly with him, and he seems utterly unaffected by her assaults, punting the boat calmly away.

"Apiya!" Sarroch shouts, still madly scrambling at the front of the boat. "Apiya!"

Throughout all this, I haven't moved. I've not been able to react, so utterly floored and numbed by what Charon said.

Only the living may leave the underworld. But I'm alive. I'm *alive.*

Aren't I?

Pree and Sarroch are still screaming my name, trying to scramble off the boat, trying to stop Charon, but I just stand there, unable to move.

Behind me I sense the mist where Eyva disappeared, except that now the pull of it is stronger. I can feel movement, warmth and other things behind me. I don't need to turn around to know that if I did, I would be hearing and seeing all kinds of things.

I don't want to see. I don't want to know. What is beyond the mist is for the dead. And I'm not dead.

"I'm alive!" I scream after the boat, finally moving, though far too late. "Charon! Come back—I'm alive, I'm..." The ferry man continues to punt the boat away. "I'm alive," I whisper.

I can't believe this is happening. I refuse to believe this is happening. I don't accept this.

And then I realise that my hands feel cold and numb, as if they've been plunged in ice this whole time.

And more to the point, I haven't taken a breath since I last shouted.

26

"I'm alive," I scream with all my might, feeling the air coming out of my mouth.

I force myself to take a deep breath in. Behind me, I feel something vast opening, and I have to actively fight against the urge to turn to it.

The boat is now barely visible, slowly being swallowed up by the mist on the river.

I take another breath. It no longer happens automatically, and I remember what Mr Sangong told me. My body has been alive because it believed it was, and now that I've been confronted with evidence that it isn't, what does that mean?

"Screw you, Charon," I shout. And that counts as another breath. I kick off my boots and breathe. I yank my top over my head, another breath. I wriggle out of my jeans. "I'm alive, and you can piss off if you think you can convince me otherwise."

I throw myself into the Styx.

The water is so cold and deep, not only does it snatch my breath away, I seize up completely and sink like a stone.

Cold, dead fingers, as soft as the mud that lines the bottom of the river, reach for me, stroking my skin, pulling me down.

I scream and swallow a bellyful of water, but I thrash my limbs until I break the surface again.

By then, the boat has completely disappeared.

"No. No!" I start to swim forward, kicking my legs, plunging one hand after the other into the water and pulling myself through it. I can feel those soft, muddy fingers tugging at my legs, brushing against my bare stomach.

I ignore them, forcing myself to breathe with each stroke. I'm alive. I'm alive. I'm *goddammed* alive!

When I finally stop, treading water, the mist is thick all around me. I have no idea which direction I've just come from, where the shore of the Styx is, or the shore of the Thames.

"Sarroch!" I yell. "Pree! Make some noise, I need direction."

The silence is absolute, save for my breathing, as I force it in and out. In and out, like a person with a body that's alive.

"Sarroch! Pree!"

Nothing.

I realise I've forgotten about possibly the most powerful person in my life. I reach up with my magic, towards the huge presence of Qinglong up there. She can guide me. She's been there for me every time I've been on the edge of destruction.

I reach higher and higher...and come up with nothing. She's not there.

Of course. This is the underworld. There is no sky here. This isn't Qinglong's realm.

I'm alone. Totally alone. More alone than I've ever been my whole life.

The thought is painfully terrifying. I'm alone and lost in the River Styx.

"Stay calm, Apiya, stay calm." Talking is good. It gives me something to hear, to focus on, and it makes me breathe.

I take the best guess I can as to the correct direction and swim forward again. "I'm coming," I announce. "I'm alive and crossing the River Styx, see if I don't."

I keep on talking to drown out the vast silence. But time passes, and I still don't see anything. I pause to tread water, turning this way and that to check and make sure I'm not missing something.

Nothing. Nothing but silence and the cold, black river.

Those cold fingers are still there. They're not aggressive, just insistent, gently tugging at me as soon as I stop moving.

They don't have to be aggressive. If I keep on like this, I'll exhaust myself, and then it won't take much to tug me below the surface. I have to know what direction to swim in, otherwise I might end up swimming the length of the river, never reaching any destination.

My teeth are chattering from cold and fear.

"Pree? Sarroch! Sarroch!!!" I realise that I'm crying. I would give anything to see them right now.

This can't be how I finish. It can't be.

"I'm alive," I wail. "I'm alive." I think of my parents. Of Chai and Hunter waiting for me back in Panong. I think of all my animals, and Zer, the pari-pari youngling. Of Mr Sangong and all my customers at the barbershop.

I have people. The dead don't have people. "I'm alive and I have people and animals to go back to!" I shout. "I'm not dead. I've never been dead." But a small traitorous voice whispers in my mind that this isn't true. My body started off as a dead baby. It was dead before my energy was infused into it.

I push the thought aside. I have to focus on being alive. I have to believe it for it to be true.

I swim forward again. My strokes are growing clumsy as I start to tire. Being tired means being alive. The dead aren't tired.

The desperate irony of it causes a bubble of hysterical laughter to rise up in my throat. If I'm tired, if my teeth are chattering and I'm crying, all that is confirmation that my body is in fact alive. I realise I no longer have to remind myself to breathe.

But what exactly is the point of that, if I'm just going to drown in the River Styx because I'll exhaust myself swimming around without finding the way back?

I don't want to die. I'm not ready. It would kill my parents.

And who will take care of Hunter when I'm gone?

"Hunter," I call. "I'm coming home to you."

I start to swim forward again.

———

I'VE BEEN SWIMMING FOR A LITTLE WHILE WHEN I HEAR A barking sound. It's so faint that for a moment I think I might have imagined it. Then it happens again. It's coming from my right.

"Hunter?" I call. "Hunter!"

Hunter, who is supposed to be my guide. I never understood what that means exactly, but that reminder makes me feel confident that it's him I'm hearing.

"Hunter! Keep barking. Good boy, Hunter. Good boy." I continue to swim in the direction of his barks.

"Sarroch?" I try. "Chai? Pree?"

Silence. The spike of panic is so sharp I briefly sink below the surface, coughing and spluttering back up.

"Hunter," I call as I spit river water back out. "Hunter!"

He barks again.

"Good boy. Hunter, my love, you have no idea how many treats and cuddles I will lavish on you when I get back."

I focus all my attention on him, reaching for him with my magic. The connection is so tenuous, it's more fragile than fingertips brushing against a single spider's thread.

But it *is* a connection. I ignore the cramp in my left leg, the exhaustion in my arms, and, gritting my teeth, continue thrashing my way forward.

"Good boy, Hunter. Such a good boy. Who is the bestest boy in the whole wide world?" I repeat this litany over and over, holding onto it like a mantra against my growing exhaustion.

And slowly, bit by bit, Hunter's bark gets more solid, louder.

"That's right, Hunter, that's right. You know I'm alive, and you want me home. I want to get back too. You hear that Charon?" I yell. "You hear me? I'm bloody well alive, and you can't trick me into staying in the underworld."

But in spite of Hunter's bark growing louder, the mist remains thick as ever.

My body's so tired, now, I'm not so much swimming as splashing, my progress forward painfully slow.

Whatever adrenaline has been propelling me forward until now is slowly leaving me. My teeth are chattering so hard it's difficult to speak.

"G-g-g-good b-b-b-boy, Hun-hunter." A few splashes forward. He barks more insistently. "I'm..alive. Alive. Good b-b-b-boy."

I fumble in the water. My limbs feel like lead that has been left in a freezer for too long. I turn onto my back to rest. "T-t-t-treats for my Hunter."

My breath should be fogging before my face from the cold, but there's nothing to see but darkness.

Nothing but those cold, soft fingers beneath me. They curl around my ankles and tug, oh-so-gently. I kick weakly. One of my legs doesn't move, the other just shifts vaguely.

The fingers return and tug again. I try to shake them off, but I'm too exhausted.

Hunter starts to bark like crazy. The fingers pull me under by the ankles very slowly. I'm dimly aware of it, but I can't seem to find the energy to kick my legs.

And then I spot it. It's faint through the mist but there, high overhead. The moon. I'm almost back to the Mundane world.

"Sarroch," I whisper. "Sarroch. Help me. Somebody help me."

The fingers tug me further, and the water closes over my head.

27

The roar is unnaturally loud, given that I'm underwater. Something large pushes me up to the surface. I cough and splutter and hold weakly to it.

Another powerful roar. It's so loud it would have made me wince from the pain of hearing it if I wasn't too exhausted for even so small a reaction.

I can feel powerful muscles working beneath me, bunching and releasing as we move swiftly through the water. My cheek is resting against wet fur. White fur, with black stripes. I curl my fingers into it.

"Sarroch," I whisper. "You came back for me."

He makes a low rumble in response.

A few moments later someone shouts "Apiya!"

That's Pree. I hear splashing. Hands grab me, steadying me on the back of Sarroch's tiger. As the water becomes shallower, he steps out of it, still carrying me on his back.

When we reach the shore, Pree carefully tugs me off, helping me down to the ground, my body shaking hard enough to rival Sarroch's plane.

The pebbles are cold and slimy against the bare skin of my back once she has me lying down, but right now it's the best feeling in the world because they're real. Solid. And when I open my eyes, I see the moon overhead clearly.

"We need an ambulance," Pree snaps. "*Now.*"

There's a flurry of movement. Warm but wet fur pushes up against me. Pree rattles off information and directions in a commanding tone, using words like 'possible hypothermia', and 'swallowed river water'.

I look up to see Charon's green eye in the darkness.

"I'm not d-d-d-dead," I manage to whisper at him.

He nods once. "I'll give you that. But you still aren't alive enough to qualify as fully part of the living."

After that, everything grows fuzzy.

———

I DRIFT IN AND OUT OF CONSCIOUSNESS A FEW TIMES. THINGS are beeping, there is a confusing amount of movement around me. Sarroch squeezes my hand. He's wearing a Spice Girls sweatshirt that's too tight for him.

The next time I come to, some kind of tube is in my throat making me gag, and I'm weakly trying to remove it. Sarroch is there again, but this time he's holding my hands in place to stop me moving. He's still wearing the Spice Girls sweatshirt.

I wake up a few more times, screaming in the dark that I'm alive, or at least trying to scream, but all that comes out is a reedy whisper.

Sarroch is there each time. So is the Spice Girls sweatshirt.

By the time I finally, properly regain consciousness, it's bright daylight. I blink a few times, my eyelids gummed together. Some machine is beeping gently to my left. A mask is covering my mouth and nose, pumping warm, humid air. Several IVs are connected to my veins. The blanket covering me from the chin down is heavy and heated.

I reach for the mask to remove it.

"Hold on. Hold on. I'll do it." Sarroch reaches over from his chair and gently removes the mask. He takes my hand. "How are you feeling?"

My throat feels too dry to speak, and he guesses that, bringing me a cup of warm water with a straw. I take a couple of small sips.

"You cannot even imagine how relieved I am to see you awake." His voice is choked.

"Probably about as shocked as I am to see you in a Spice Girls sweatshirt," I croak.

He's still wearing it, above a pair of green hospital scrubs.

Sarroch laughs and takes my hand. "I was naked after shifting back to human form—I ripped my own clothes apart when I shifted to tiger. This was all Priscilla had in her car to lend me once the ambulance had arrived. That and a pair of lycra running shorts. I think I traumatised several nurses—the scrubs are a vast improvement."

"I doubt anyone was traumatised," I manage.

I think that's all the banter I have in me right now.

"They pumped your stomach, which was full of river water. You've been treated for the hypothermia and you're on antibiotics to help your body fight whatever nasties you'd have picked up in the Thames."

I nod once. "Will I—"

"They expect you to make a complete recovery. There's nothing to worry about."

"Pree…"

"She's outside. They wouldn't let both of us be in the room with you, but she's been waiting outside, and she's been coming to check on you regularly. I'll go get her shortly."

He takes a shaky breath. "Apiya, do you think you're strong enough for me to formally introduce you to my tiger? Not like what happened in Panong. Properly this time." One of his hands comes to my cheek, and he rubs his thumb gently against my skin. "You can't imagine what it did to me to watch you alone on the shore of the river Styx while the boat left, and I was powerless to get back to you. I don't ever want this to happen again. I won't risk losing you. I know we have until the full moon tonight, but I don't want to chance it. Once the mating bond is fully in place, it will bring you security from the Mayak, but it will also ensure that what happened at the Styx can't happen again. I'll be able to use our link to keep you safe." He's gripping my hands so tightly in his now, it almost hurts. "I can't lose you. I can't... I can't go through that again."

His eyes are intense as they search mine.

"I don't want to lose you either," I tell him. "And yes, give me a bit of time to be a bit more with it, and I would really like to properly meet your tiger."

28

Sarroch leaves me briefly to go organise a few things, which means Pree can come in. I haven't been awake long, but I'm feeling better and better with each moment that passes.

I grin at the sight of her.

"I can't believe you gave him a Spice Girls sweatshirt." Pree was embarrassingly passionate about the girl band as a teenager.

"I swear, in the moment there was so much going on, that's all I found in the boot of my car." Then her eyes gleam mischievously. "Later on, once I knew for sure you were fine, I went back to my car, and I found a long-sleeved, tie-dye men's top that I bought to cut up into something funky. I could have given it to him to swap out the Spice Girls sweatshirt, but I thought seeing it would cheer you up when you woke up."

"You guessed right."

Her cheerful expression fades away. "I'm so glad you're okay. I thought we were going to lose you."

"You and me both. But I'm alive." I say it with conviction.

"Oh, here." She fishes out a folded piece of paper from her back pocket. "Oops, it got a bit wrinkled." As does most paperwork when it comes into contact with Pree. She unfolds it and smooths it out with one hand. "I got one of the nurses to write out a certificate of life. You know how they write a death certificate? Well, I got her to do the same thing but to confirm that you're alive. That way next time some moron, supernatural or not, tries to tell you that you're not, you can wave that in their face."

It's a small, stupid thing, really. At the end of the day, who needs a piece of paper to let them know that they're alive? But the gesture touches something deep inside me, and I find myself choking up. I run my finger on the wrinkled paper, over my name and the confirmation that earlier this morning a medical professional confirmed that I was alive.

"They checked all your vitals and confirmed—proper medical confirmed—that you're alive," Pree taps a finger on the certificate.

"Thanks, Pree. I can't believe you managed to get someone to do this." The certificate is the real deal, with a proper hospital stamp and everything.

"I just stood at the nurse's station singing 'Spice Up Your Life' over and over again until someone agreed to write the certificate to shut me up."

I look from the wrinkled piece of paper up at my oldest friend. I don't think many things sum up Pree as well as this.

"I also need to ask you about all those injuries you have," she says. "I trust your judgement, and Sarroch seems like a good guy, but looks like you had a lot of cuts, and your shoulder got cut up quite bad, although the doctors say it's healing well. What's that all about? You safe?"

"Yeah. I'm fine. There's nothing for you to worry about. Not now we've taken care of the hungry ghost."

"So long as you're sure."

"I am."

Sarroch returns soon after, confirming that he's secured total privacy for my hospital room for the next couple of hours—no doctor or nurse will be attempting to come in. Just to be safe, though, Pree announces that she'll be standing guard at the door with her cricket bat.

"Although I will be within hearing range," she warns. "So if there is to be hanky panky, it better be quiet."

Sarroch gravely informs her that 'hanky panky isn't part of the formal weretiger mating bond ritual'. I swallow down the urge to laugh at so ridiculous a sentence.

Pree heads off and closes the door. Once Sarroch and I are alone, I ask him what the ritual will entail.

"Well, normally it's quite a beautiful ceremony. If we had been able to do this in the werecat's realm, everyone would have gathered beneath the purple canopy. There would have been music, readings from some of our old, sacred texts, and Pragya would have conducted the ritual..."

"And the ritual is...?"

Sarah grimaces. "We normally have a lot of stuff around it, but when you boil it down..."

"Yes?"

"We each have to consume a small part of each other's flesh."

"Ugh, *what*? Seriously?"

"Seriously. In order for it to work, both me and my tiger need to have chosen you as a mate, of course. Then the magic can take place. If not, it's just a weird form of cannibalism."

"Wait... Does that mean your tiger has chosen me?"

"Didn't you hear him roaring to try to help you find your way to us, back at the river?"

"That was him the whole time?"

Sarroch nods. "We got back to the Thames, but I could still hear you somewhere in the distance. I couldn't see you, but my tiger sees and hears better. I shifted, and he went plunging into the river, swimming around and roaring for you, hoping you'd hear him and be able to find us."

"For most of it I heard it as Hunter barking."

"Yes, I felt Hunter too, actually. You did something that has a link to him, back in the underworld, didn't you?"

"I did. Um, so when did your tiger change his mind about me?" I feel weirdly shy and vulnerable asking that question.

"I don't think he actually got to make a decision about you until now. Until after what you did in the underworld. It's only now that things are different that I'm realising just how badly he was affected by the hungry ghost. I had grown so closed-off, so disconnected... And so had he. I guess it was such a gradual thing that neither of us really realised what was happening. That was the thing that was the most confusing. Neither of us really understood why he had such a problem with you. Him least of all. Because he didn't. That was the hungry ghost. Since it had its origins in Eyva, I guess it was jealous in its own way."

"Can you and your tiger talk to each other?"

"Sort of. And he didn't fully understand why he was so angry and repulsed when he met you back at my place, because until then, he actually quite liked you from what he experienced through me. I tried to rationalise it in terms of the loss of Eyva, but it obviously wasn't that. And then out of nowhere, when we were in the hunt and we were racing alongside you on your motorbike, he felt so joyful and happy..."

"And then the hungry ghost took over and had him cut me off." It's all making sense now.

"Exactly, that's what I figure must have happened. But now that my tiger is free, it will be different for you to meet him...properly. That's the final requirement that is needed before we can go through the mating bond ritual. We've already slept together, so that is the connection to me. We need the connection to my tiger, which will happen when you meet him officially and he chooses you, and then we can do the mating bond ritual."

"Okay." I'm feeling really, really nervous. And I wish we didn't have to do this with me in a hospital bed.

"You'll have to close your eyes. Normally, I'd go somewhere else to shift. It's really not the done thing to shift in sight of a potential mate just before a formal introduction. But obviously it's not really possible in the hospital. I can't see that the doctors and nurses would be okay with a huge sabre-tooth tiger walking through the corridors."

I close my eyes and do my best not to pretend I can't hear bones breaking and joints popping.

To Sarroch's credit, he doesn't make a single sound other than a soft grunt about halfway through the transformation. I keep my eyes closed until I hear a soft rumble.

Seriously, I don't think I'll ever get used to the sight of Sarroch's tiger. If there is a more magnificent creature out in the world, I have yet to encounter it. His fur is a pure, gleaming white, the stripes a perfect inky black in a mesmerising pattern. His head is framed by a very faint ruff, a lot smaller than what I saw on Eyva's tigress. The two huge sabre-tooth canines glisten, but they look more beautiful now and less sharp and scary.

But the most striking aspect of him are his glacier-pale eyes. They are wide,now, and staring at me, but there's a gentleness to them that I haven't seen before.

He comes to the side of the bed—he doesn't need to stand on his hind legs for his head to be level with mine—and he makes a soft, chuffing sound as he brings his head to rest against mine. Tigers can't purr, so that's their equivalent.

I reach a hesitant hand up to the ruff of fur at his neck. It's soft and silky and so dense my fingers disappear within it. He chuffs again.

Sura Taoray.

The name just pops into my head. I straighten up to look at him. "Sura Taoray? Is that your name?"

He chuffs and lets out a low, pleased rumble.

"Sura," I repeat, getting used to the name. "Sura and Sarroch. Sarroch and Sura. Twin souls."

A low rumble of agreement. I grin and bury both hands in his fur, stroking behind his ears, realising now what Sarroch meant when he said I still hadn't been introduced to his tiger. "It's really good to finally, properly, meet you, Sura."

29

I wish I could say that the mating bond ritual was a beautiful thing. I wish I could say that something amazing washed over the both of us, that the air was thick with mystical, spiritual energy. That the heavens wept, and the earth moved, and that—

There's just no way around it—it was grim. You just can't make having to ingest even the tiniest scrap of your mate's flesh anything other than really disturbing. I'm not vegetarian, but I've been toying with the idea for a long time, so this is really beyond the pale for me.

After he changed back to human, Sarroch produced one of my cutthroat razors. "It seemed only right we do it with your razor, rather than with something generic like a hospital scalpel."

I really appreciate the fact that he put thought into it, but to be brutally honest, it didn't really do much to make the whole thing less horrid.

Sarroch sliced two teeny tiny little scraps of skin from each of us. It was painful, but not unbearable. I couldn't look as he ingested the part of me, and I had to close my eyes and open my mouth so that I didn't see what I was eating. Even then, I gagged a couple of times before I managed to swallow the scrap.

So yeah, that part was grim.

However, as soon as I swallow, it becomes magical.

I can feel something soft and warm, something that feels like golden afternoon light connecting Sarroch, Sura, and I. A wave of magic washes over me—over us both. I realise that I can sense everything Sarroch and Sura sense, and they can sense what I do. There is a feeling of total, perfect completion. Like the three of us were always meant to be a triangle, and we are finally joined in the way we are meant to be.

Time seems to grow suspended as the three of us are caught up in the complete perfection of the moment.

And then it fades back. I can still sense the soft undercurrent of magic linking us, but I can no longer sense what they sense, and vice versa.

Sarroch takes a deep, deep breath, and for a moment he looks overcome with relief. "And now you are safe."

He bends down to the bed and gives me a long, slow kiss.

"Hmm, being safe isn't half bad," I comment as he pulls back.

He laughs huskily.

"So what is a mating bond like, exactly?" I ask. "Will we be able to sense where the other one is, or something like that?"

"A mating bond is as unique as the individuals who make it up. It will be for us to discover over time what our bond does and how it works. We're likely to have some quirks that others don't experience, since you aren't a shifter. There are normally four souls making up the mating bond, but we only have three. So I'm sure that as with everything you're involved in, it will make for an interesting experience."

I snort. "You know what, I think I've had enough 'interesting' to last me a lifetime. For now, I'd happily settle for easy, relaxed, and as you said before, safe."

He nods gravely. "I agree. Which is why I started making arrangements, although I was waiting for the mating bond to be fully into effect before I set them all in motion."

"Arrangements?"

"Well, now that we are mated, you'll want to move in. Would you prefer me to have my people take care of everything so that when you arrive all of your things already in my house, or would you rather be there to oversee the process?"

"Um...what? Moving?"

"Yes. To my place."

"And what exactly makes you think that we should move into your place?"

"Well, I only figured that since my place is bigger and better than yours—"

I raise an eyebrow at him. "Better? Does your place have a tomato trellis that's at the perfect distance from the wall so that Fergie can climb up before he wedges himself between the two? Or a pond with the perfect rocky hiding spot for Frank during the hot afternoons so he can remain cool and moist? There's the patch of sunlight that Hunter likes to sunbathe in, and all the little habits that Zer has picked up —she has her routines and comforts and they all require *my* courtyard... The only thing I would concede is that you probably have a better quality record player than me."

Sarroch frowns. "Okay... I have to admit, I hadn't considered the possibility that you might want to stay in your house. I thought women tended to like nice big houses." He runs a hand through his hair, obviously thinking things through. "Okay. I will see about making arrangements to move myself into your house, although, of course, I have far too many things to fit into your space. But I could potentially commission a small Mayak space to be built within your house. It would take time, but I think I could get it done—"

I grab his hand before he starts to plan the complete transformation of my little house. "Sarroch, who says we have to move in together, anyway? I'm not sure I'm particularly ready for it."

He looks as taken aback as I was by his announcement that I was about to move house. "But we're mated."

"I know. And we've been through a lot together. But Sarroch, we haven't even been on a first proper date yet." I raise a hand to interrupt him. "No, the time you took me to the Panongian opera doesn't count. We didn't speak for the whole evening, and it wasn't a date, but a rather over-the-top gesture of apology. Plus, it was pretty clear you didn't like me much back then." I still have my other hand in his and I twine my fingers in his. "We have all the time in the world. I think it would be nice for us to at least have a few dinners out, you know, do the regular dating thing before we go for the full on living-together-discovering-all-of-each-other's-irritating-little-habits."

"I'm sure you don't have any irritating habits," he says gallantly.

I give him a look. "Sarroch, that is a lovely sentiment, the kind bandied about by bad rom-coms, but it's far from true. I have plenty of annoying habits, and so do you. Look, I know we're kind of doing things the wrong way round. Like getting married before having a first date, but then again, nothing about our relationship so far has been normal."

Sarroch mulls this over as if it's an extraordinary concept. "You want to date."

I smile widely. "Yes. Dating. It's supposed to be nice. Very nice."

He grimaces. "I don't know that I have ever been on what humans consider a date. Not in the modern way of thinking. Not in this century or the last one."

"Well, lucky for you, I have been on plenty of dates. Consider this me officially asking you out, and I will organise our first proper date."

"Wait a minute. I know enough to know that the man should do the asking and the taking for the first date."

I pat his hand. "Not in the twenty-first century. The first date's mine. You can ask me out for our second date."

Sarroch smiles. "Okay, it's a deal. I can do that." And then he leans in and kisses me again.

Yep, dating isn't half bad.

30

There's one more thing we need to cover. For all my 'let's take it slow' speech, my next suggestion flies in the face of that. But I just can't leave England without going to visit my parents.

And after everything that happened, it would feel all kinds of wrong to not bring Sarroch along so they can meet him.

"I really don't know about this," Sarroch says. "I'm not sure I could look either of them in the eye, not after everything I've put you through."

"Sarroch, we're going to clear the air about this, and after that, you have to promise me that you will stop worrying about it. You did not put me through anything—the hungry ghost, a nasty parasite born of your shame and grief and pain, did. I've already forgiven you everything, even though there is nothing to forgive."

"I doubt your parents will see it that way."

"My parents don't know about that, and I don't plan on telling them." And I'm not lying. I don't really see the point in upsetting them, because it will be upsetting for them to hear the kind of danger I was in, and I also don't particularly want to create a situation where they'll see Sarroch unfavourably before they've had a chance to get to know him properly.

Sarroch shakes his head. "I still don't know whether it's a good idea."

"Please, Sarroch. It really would mean a lot to me if you met them."

He sighs. "If it means a lot to you, how can I argue with that?"

"An excellent point." I smile at him. "It will be fine. More than fine. You'll probably enjoy meeting them. They're amazing."

———

Now that our mating bond is official, Sarroch no longer needs to keep his presence in Europe hidden since there's nothing the Mayak Elders can do to me. We got the mating bond within the specified deadline, which means I am officially part of the Mayak, and all their laws apply to me. Something which is seriously satisfying.

That should, in theory, mean that Sarroch is free to rent out a car to drive us over to my parents' house.

But Pree won't hear of it, insisting that she will play chauffeur to the 'newlyweds'.

Sarroch makes a decent attempt at talking her out of it but gives up when she points out that her offer isn't entirely selfless—she's feeling nostalgic and she wants me to help her dye her hair purple in my parents' bathroom, like we did when we were kids.

Sarroch is turning out to be quite the softy—the moment Pree mentions nostalgia, all his arguing stops.

Although he does go and buy himself a new set of clothes, which is wise. No matter how open-minded and relaxed my parents are, it's true that hospital scrubs and a too-small Spice Girls hoodie are hardly the way to make an impression.

We are pulling up outside of their house in Pree's turd on wheels, the engine wheezing in the usual way.

"What if they don't like me?" Sarroch asks suddenly. He's looking downright dapper in a crisp white shirt and a gorgeously fitting pair of jeans. Although he went for understated on the clothes, he didn't quite have the same restraint in buying gifts for my parents. There is a veritable cornucopia of flowers, assorted luxury chocolate truffles in a pretty but huge gold and light blue box, and a bottle of expensive port after I let slip that my dad is a fan of the stuff.

It's highly amusing and more than a little touching to see a powerful weretiger getting so nervous at the thought of meeting two harmless, middle-aged humans. Although to be fair to him, my mother's strength of will could be used as the front plate of a bulldozer. But he doesn't know that. Yet.

"They put up with me, don't they?" I joke.

"Like that's hard," he replies.

Pree laughs. "You'll be fine, Sarroch. They like me, so I think it's fair to say that their standards are set rather low."

"She's right," I reply. "Also, don't forget that you're a Mayak, so my father already thinks that you're the most amazing person in the world. You'd have to do something as crazy as sell me into slavery for my father to think poorly of you. As for my mum, she'll think the world of you so long as I'm happy. And I am."

———

MY PARENTS LIVE IN A LOVELY LITTLE HOUSE ON THE outskirts of London. It's a cosy, messy house, with books everywhere, most of them well-thumbed and dog-eared. Art and hand-crafted objects from around the world decorate shelves and sideboards, a reminder of how much my parents travelled before they settled back in England when I was a kid.

My mum has an eclectic taste in artwork, so alongside African masks are rather crazy modern prints. The seating in the living room is all very much focused on comfort— wide chairs with plump cushions that do their best to swallow you up when you sit down, perfect for curling up in with a book.

Introducing my parents to Sarroch goes much as I had expected. Dad falls over himself in his eagerness to shake Sarroch's hand, which is awkward given the mountain of gifts he's cradling in his arms.

Mum takes it all off his hands, informing him that she likes a man who comes bearing chocolates. Sarroch has a split second to look relieved before Dad whisks him away into the living room while peppering him with the *numerous* questions he has prepared.

Mum takes Pree and me into the kitchen where she's been bustling up a storm all afternoon, as evidenced by the sheer amount of food she's prepared. It also looks like a tornado has been in the kitchen, pulling out every pot, pan, and utensil, scattering them across the counter.

It's a mystery to us both that I turned into such a neat freak.

The kitchen is bright and sunny, light pouring in through the skylight overhead and through the open doors that lead out to the garden. The weather is cooperating, giving us a rare day of sunshine.

Comforting, familiar smells fill the kitchen.

"You made bread and butter pudding," I exclaim. My mum makes the *best* bread and butter pudding with lots of nutmeg and cinnamon and raisins. Proper comfort food.

I go to stick my spoon in it, but before I can, she grabs me into a hug tight enough to crush my ribs. "I'm so glad you're okay," she whispers. She releases me and kisses me on each cheek, holding my face in her hands. Her eyes are bright with unshed tears.

She might not have known about what went down in Bhutan and London, but she knows about Chizu and my trial, which is more than enough to get her upset already.

"Mum, you're going to make me cry."

"And me," Pree echoes.

"Now, none of that," Mum says briskly, quickly wiping her own eyes. "That wasn't the aim." She starts bustling about the kitchen once more. I tuck into the pudding. It's gooey and vanilla-ey, and full of spices, and just tastes like childhood.

"This is a happy, happy day," Mum says. "I can't believe we *finally* get to meet one of Apiya's boyfriends."

Pree sits herself on one of the high stools at the kitchen island and grabs a mini pork pie. "That's because it's the first time Api's dating someone that wouldn't be mortifying to introduce to you guys."

I fling a carrot stick at her head, and she ducks.

———

WE GET BACK TO THE LIVING ROOM, WHERE THINGS FOLLOW the expected course of action. My dad has enough self-control to remember to ask for Sarroch's consent before recording their conversation about some obscure piece of

Panongian folklore while Mum pushes masses of food and tea on everyone. No is not a word she comprehends.

In his eagerness to get the recording going, Dad spills his tea all over his smart phone which promptly dies.

Sarroch gallantly offers to use his own phone to record the conversation, promising that he will email the file over as soon as they're done talking. Isn't he classy?

Once they get going with their conversation, Sarroch's original stiffness and awkwardness melts away as Dad becomes more and more animated and enthusiastic about the subject at hand. Right now, he'll be as happy as a pig in a wallow. I'd actually wager that he has completely forgotten that he is meeting my boyfriend—I mean, my mate. I'll have to get used to saying that.

"If you're all settled here with Api's boyfriend," Pree says to Mum, "Would you mind me stealing her for a hair dying session in your bathroom?"

My father looks up in surprise. "Boyfriend?" He looks at Sarroch and his gaze clears. "Oh yes, that's right. You're Apiya's boyfriend. Apologies, Sarroch. I was so caught up in our discussion…"

Sarroch raises a pacifying hand. "That's quite all right. I was enjoying it every bit as much as you. And it's a lot less awkward than the whole 'what are your intentions with my daughter' thing."

"Yes, because what I really want to know is what exactly *were* your intentions when, in the seventh century…" And the conversation goes off again.

I grin. "Pree, I think we're safe to go upstairs."

"You do that, girls. I'll keep an eye on both of them," Mum says.

"Don't worry about the bathroom. I'll make sure there are no stains," I tell her.

"Apiya, I have learnt by now that it is pointless to expect you to leave a room anything but spotless."

True that.

———

WE ARRIVE AT HEATHROW AIRPORT IN MUCH THE SAME WAY that we left it—escorted by Pree in her car.

Except that this time, Pree's hair isn't vomit green but a beautifully bright purple. It looks all the more cool with the shaved side of her head.

I used my magic to give her hair a bit of oomph, helping it shed the dry frizz it picked up from so many years of being abused with cheap chemical dyes. Now it's back to how I remember it as a teenager, thick and wavy and luscious, tumbling down the right side of her face in a gorgeous purple waterfall.

To go with her new hair, she's wearing a hot pink T-shirt that reads 'screw world peace, I want a pony' over a pair of plaid trousers with the left leg covered in red and black checks, while the right leg is a black-and-white. Chains are looped around her hips, and her trousers are tucked into her Doc Martens. Classic London punk attire from the waist down, undefinable Pree-type fashion from the waist up.

"It was twenty pence at a charity shop," Pree tells Sarroch in reply to his question as to what on earth possessed her to get that T-shirt. "You can get such great stuff in charity shops, plus it's so cheap."

As she walks us to the departure gate, I find myself growing choked at the thought of leaving her. I hug her fiercely. "Thank you for everything, Pree. We wouldn't have made it without you."

"Well, that's what friends are for."

I break the hug. "And Pree, please don't do anything dangerous. *Please*. The world of magic isn't to be messed with."

"I know," she replies soothingly.

"If there's anything, anything at all—even if it's just that you've got some weird feeling, or something bothers you, you *call me*. Okay?"

"I promise, if you promise you'll keep in touch properly this time, and tell me everything that's going on with you in Panong. Not just the watered-down 'Mundane' version." She uses air quotes around the word mundane—she definitely wasn't pleased to realise that she's part of a group of people referred to as that. After all, Pree is anything but mundane.

"I also very much enjoyed getting to know you, Priscilla," Sarroch says in his slightly formal way.

"Stiff, awkward, not displaying any real emotion? I love it!" Pree hoots. "You *must* be British." And with that, she slings both arms around him in a hug, and kisses him on both cheeks. "I'm so glad I got to know you. You look after Api, now, or you'll answer to me."

And then it's time for Sarroch and I to head to our gate. Thankfully, we're flying in a commercial, *modern* plane, all the way to Panong.

Not only that, but Sarroch has pulled out his 'I'm a CEO credit card' and bought us business class tickets.

As I sit down in my comfortable seat with a cabin crew member bringing me a small glass of champagne, I can confirm that this is a vastly, vastly superior way of travelling than by private plane.

EPILOGUE

As much as I enjoyed discovering Bhutan, the werecat realm, and as much as I enjoyed being back in England for a time, nothing matches the warm surge of happiness I get at the sight of my little house in Old Town.

I'm so excited to be reunited with Chai and Hunter and my menagerie, to see how my little pineapple plant is going, and just to be home once again.

Not only that, but now that I'm Sarroch's mate and all the issues with the Mayak have been resolved, I'm free to go back to work at Mr Sangong's barbershop again. I've really missed my job and my regulars. It'll be so good to get back to normal.

That's all I want for now. A bit of normality. To just slip back into my routine of going to work at night, caring for my animals, hanging out with Chai, and practising Muay Thai during the day.

I smile to myself. Although now I guess I also need to put aside time for seeing Sarroch, which is a pretty cool change. Our first official date is two days from now, and I've got to plan what we're going to do. I don't know what it will be yet, but I intend to make it an amazing first date. We deserve it.

For now, I step under the covered area by my front door, reaching out to pat my motorbike, happy to see it still parked as I left it, safe and sound. I unsling my backpack from my shoulder, fishing around in it to locate my house keys.

Chai opens the door before I can finish unlocking it, and he's barged out of the way by Hunter. He's so excited he lets out a small stream of pee as he rushes to me, only just missing Chai's shoe.

"Sorry," I tell Chai as I crouch down. "Give me a second to say hi to Hunter."

Chai grins. "Take your time."

There are a lot of 'who's a good boy, who's the bestest boy in the whole world, who's going to get ALL the treats?' and much stroking from me, while Hunter throws himself at me over and over again, whining and wiggling his entire body for all he's worth.

I'm always very careful to make a big deal of Hunter's greetings. He has separation anxiety from his previous family abandoning him in normal times, but if he was somehow aware of me being close to shifting over to being dead, that would have been awful for him.

So he deserves all the attention I can give him. And of course he most definitely helped save the day once again. For a dog that a professional dog trainer called pathologi-cally untrainable, he has saved the day in dangerous situa-tions numerous times by now.

When Hunter finally starts to calm down, I stand back up and turn to Chai to give him a hug. I pull away and make a show of looking at the floor around him. "You didn't wet yourself at my arrival? You're such a fake, pretending you're actually excited to see me, when you don't even care enough to wee on the floor."

Chai laughs. "Next to Hunter's displays, we're all fakes. But I am *very* relieved to see you back looking healthy and happy, pumpkin."

"And I'm glad to be back."

"I'll give you a moment to check on the rest of your animals and get over the flight, and then I want details, darling." He raises an eyebrow and gives me a perfectly salacious look. "I particularly want all the *juicy* details."

Now it's my turn to laugh. "I won't be getting *that* juicy."

"Petal, my social life is worse than the Sahara. Next to my love life, the Sahara is a fertile valley filled with a rich biodiversity of plants and animals. I need to live vicariously through you, especially since you are now mated to the *hottest* Mayak in Panong."

I can't help but grin at that. "He is the hottest Mayak, isn't he? And now he's all mine." That thought makes me genuinely happy, and more than a little smug.

Something pushes against my ankle and I looked down to find Tim rubbing his face against my legs.

"So you came back," he says nonchalantly.

"Don't go overboard in showing how happy you are to see me," I tell him.

"Surely you aren't confusing me with the brainless fur ball? Anyway, it was clear to anyone with two neurons to spare that you'd make it back, in some form or another, so why bother getting excited at the obvious?"

Ah, cats. They sure know how to make you feel special.

He sniffs my legs. "By the way, your smell is much improved now that you are an honorary member of the felines."

"You can smell that?" I ask him.

"Of course. Obviously, you still smell like a vastly inferior creature, but you've managed to elevate yourself from the dredge of the world that are humans to the dredge of feline society, which is a vast, vast improvement."

I laugh.

"You'll be pleased to know that Tim was a big help," Chai says.

"Shut it," the cat hisses. "You say another word and I'll gouge your eyes out."

Chai rolls his eyes at me.

"Why don't you come with me to my courtyard," I suggest to Chai. "I want to check on everyone out there."

Chai and I have already spoken through messages and video calls, so I know that everyone is fine but still, it's nice to check on them.

We cross my living room and then go through my kitchen. Everything is just as I left it, all neat and tidy and organised, without so much as a wayward tea towel on the counter. I breathe in the familiar smells of my home-made floor cleaner mixed with the myriad of smells from my extensive spice cabinet.

Chai has been amazing in making sure that my little house was well looked after while I was gone.

I squeeze his hand. "Thank you."

"It was my pleasure, pet. And it was easy to do, in the end. I was a bit worried about Hunter, at first. I don't need to tell you just how difficult he found it for you to not be around."

I grimace. "Yeah... I thought that in time his separation anxiety would become less, but that doesn't seem to be the case."

"That's what I was going to tell you before." Chai drops

his voice to a whisper. "Tim stayed with him the whole time. Whether I brought Hunter to my studio with me or whether he was here, Tim was pretty much always by his side to comfort him."

"Really?"

Chai grins. "Tim threatened all manner of gruesome deaths on me if I was to tell anyone about it. He also claimed he would deny everything."

I snort with laughter. "That does sound like Tim."

Chai sobers up. "There's one more thing, by the way. It started while you were on the plane."

"It started?"

"I don't know if it's anything—I don't know enough about pari-pari younglings. But Zer has just been acting a little bit... odd. Nothing major, nothing that got me massively worried, but it might just be worth keeping an eye on her... Or him. I really don't know how you can tell her gender. Or his."

I shrug "It just seems really obvious to me... But that's good to know. I'll go check on her now, and on Fergie and all the others, and we'll see what's going on."

We step out into my little courtyard, and I take a deep breath, inhaling the flowers' perfume. Fergie the tortoise has wedged himself between the trellis and the wall. My rabbits are snacking on a bunch of carrot peels. When my guinea pig catches sight of me, he excitedly squeaks 'lettuce' in morse code. Frank the frog is nowhere to be seen, hiding in his moist hideout.

Zer is sitting in my pond with one bird perched on her head among hair that currently looks like brittle straw. The pond's water reaches up to her chest, and what skin is visible is the mottled colour of algae-covered stones.

As far as I can tell, all seems normal.

Maybe there is something wrong with Zer, and then again maybe Chai is just over thinking—he's not as used to her as I am. Maybe I have another crisis brewing on my hands, or maybe it's nothing.

It doesn't matter. For now, it's just damn good to be home.

THE END FOR NOW

———

PRISCILLA IS NEWLY UNEMPLOYED THANKS TO HER IMPULSIVE streak, and now the proud owner of a rescued hyena, also thanks to said streak. But when she stumbles upon a magical turf war, let's just say that things get a bit... hairy.

GO TO HTTPS://CELINEJEANJEANBOOKS.COM/PRODUCTS/ LAUGHING-AT-MAGIC and sink your teeth into Laughing at Magic.

———

Meanwhile, Apiya goes on her first proper date with Sarroch. Except that soon after she ends up drugged and chained, and forced to collaborate with Yue to escape. Which is a bit like trying to cuddle a rabid dog.

Want to find out how she fares? Go to https:// celinejeanjeanbooks.com/products/changed-by-trust to get your hands on the last instalment of the series, Changed by Trust.

ALSO BY CELINE JEANJEAN

If you want something to read in the mean time, you can dive into a whole new world that's like a mix of Victorian London and South East Asia. Discover a new cast of quirky characters, follow along their adventures and their banter, and escape into a **complete** 9 book series!

The gang's made up of:

- A skinny pickpocket with dreadlocks, a cheeky grin, and a smart mouth

- A foppish assassin with a fear of blood

- A handsome, elite fighter, master of the sardonic raised eyebrow

- A smuggler with a drinking problem and a propensity for brawling

- And a no-nonsense, heavily tattooed female machinist, trying to keep them all in line

Can they complete their missions without getting caught, killed, and without arguing?

The latter is by far the most problematic....

Check out the series over at http://celinejeanjean.com/viper-urchin/

* 9 7 8 2 4 9 2 5 2 3 2 9 8 *